CATCHING THE COWGIRL

LACY WILLIAMS

PROLOGUE

1903 - Philadelphia

"You're going out early."

Adam Cartwright had been heading through the foyer but stopped at the voice from the darkened library. Where—?

There. His brother Reggie sat in his wheeled chair, half-hidden behind a sofa. Adam would've passed by the room without ever seeing him if Reggie hadn't spoken.

"Does your nurse know you're down here?" Adam asked. Reggie had been wheelchair bound for near fifteen years. He rarely came downstairs anymore, mostly staying confined to his rooms.

"Where are you going?" Reggie shoved the wheels of his chair almost angrily, rounding the sofa.

Where are you going? It was an echo of the younger

brother who had once followed Adam everywhere. Even that last, fateful day.

Adam blinked away the memories.

A shaft of moonlight had fallen over Reggie, and Adam could see his eyes were bloodshot. He stank of being unwashed. And there was a tremble in his hand where it gripped the wheel.

"Have you been down here all night? I'll ring for Miss P—" What was her name? Adam could never remember. Powers? Peters?

"Don't bother. She left, and she's not coming back."

"Don't think you're rid of me so easily." Soft yellow illumination lit the front hall as a slender woman wearing an apron bustled out of the kitchen and past Adam. Obviously, she'd been listening at the door.

Some nameless emotion crossed Reggie's expression but was quickly blanked.

"You stink," Miss P. said in her brisk, no-nonsense manner. Frankly, Adam was surprised she'd lasted six months.

Adam had barely spoken to his brother in all that time. Reggie stayed locked away, and Adam couldn't bear his company. Not after what Adam had done.

This was not the time for self-recrimination. He had a very short window before he had to be back at the newspaper.

He slipped out of the house as Miss P. hustled his brother away to bed.

An hour later, the sun was up, and Adam was

standing on an expansive green lawn, well back from the estate house.

"Hallo, you." His friend Frank extended a hand. "It's been too long. I hardly recognize you."

Adam took the hand, smiling and shaking his head when Frank shook it with far too much enthusiasm. "It's only been a couple of months," Adam said.

"Try eighteen."

"No!"

"That's far too long to go without seeing your blood brother." Frank was joking, wearing a hearty smile, but Adam heard the undertone of seriousness in his voice.

Adam rolled his shoulders beneath his suit coat. He'd been busy chasing stories for Father. The last time Frank had been in Philadelphia, Adam had been on assignment in New York City. But eighteen months? Where had the time gone?

Adam and Frank's parents had been friends for decades. The boys had been all of eight when they'd pricked their thumbs with a dull pocketknife and sworn a brother's loyalty to each other.

That had been fourteen year ago, a lifetime for Adam. More. Their swearing ceremony had been mere months before Reggie's accident.

Adam didn't want to think about the darkness he'd left behind at home on Warburton Street. He had a few hours of freedom from the desk this morning, and he intended to make the most of it.

"Where is she?" he asked.

"Ah. The truth comes out." Frank didn't sound

perturbed in the least as he inclined his head toward the dirt track that bisected the rolling green grass. "You didn't come to see your blood brother after all. You came for her."

The *her* was a sleek chestnut mare currently being led toward them by a short, whip-thin man.

"She's incredible." Adam couldn't keep the admiration out of his voice. The mare was muscled with clean lines. She'd been brushed so her coat had a gorgeous sheen. "Where did you find her?"

"A farm in Kentucky. She's too rough for this year's Preakness, but next year..." Frank nodded, and the jockey climbed into the exercise saddle and reined the horse to the dirt track that Adam knew made up a quarter mile circle in the otherwise empty field.

The horse shifted, and Adam almost missed the moment she burst into motion, it happened so quickly.

He squinted against the morning sunlight, not wanting to miss one breath of the display. The mare's long stride ate up the track. Each beat of her hooves against the soft dirt took only the fleetest second. It was as if she were flying.

It was beautiful.

This sight, Adam could never hope to capture behind a desk. The breathless beauty of a horse racing not because she was forced, but because she lived for these moments.

Like another *she* had.

For one moment, he felt the wind cool against his face, heard an echo of laughter, and was back in

BelAnders Park with Breanna White of the Bear Creek, Wyoming, Whites.

He'd been instantly smitten by the girl—for she had been a girl then—who would challenge him to race when he'd been surrounded by a group of friends. Her wild beauty had captivated him. And then she'd disappeared, presumably to return home to the West.

Three years, and he still wondered what might've happened if he'd abandoned his horse and his friends and followed her through the city streets.

Nothing. Nothing would've happened. She'd been a girl, a teenager really, but still in the last throes of childhood.

And he was rooted here in Philadelphia. Chained to the *Daily Explorer*. Entrenched in his mother's social machinations.

Frank's mare rounded the last curve and past the two men, sand flying even as the jockey slowed and then walked her again around the track.

"So...?"

"She's worth her weight in gold," Adam told his friend.

Frank punched a fist into the air. "I knew it," he crowed. "I knew it the moment I laid eyes on her. You've the best eye for horseflesh I know. We'll be taking home the Stakes next year."

Adam clapped his friend on the back, laughing as he spun dreams out, the same dreams Adam had once dared to hope for.

Two hours later, Adam was hunkered down over

the battle-scarred desk where Father had pigeon-holed him two years ago. The *Explorer* office bustled around him, other reporters banging away at their typewriters or muttering in conversation with each other. Typesetters worked on tonight's edition that would hit the streets tomorrow morning before dawn.

Father hadn't known the freedom Adam would find in writing, even if it was only a window cracked open occasionally. Not the door meant for escape.

Across the office, a telephone rang. Adam's typewriter seemed to almost glare at him, waiting for something meaningful to pour from his fingers onto the page.

It rarely did.

Adam's gaze flicked to his father's office. Maybe today he would march in there and quit. He struck the fanciful thought. Father would disown him.

Father's light was off, the door closed tightly. Had he gone home early?

No.

More likely, he'd run off to some important meeting with his cronies. Father was never home early, not once in all the years Adam could remember. He worked from dawn until dusk, sometimes later. Adam saw him more often at the parties Mother either hosted or attended than at the supper table.

Father wanted Adam to be just like him. To take over the paper, eventually. It had been Adam's duty since birth.

Adam could think of no worse fate. Oh, he knew

the business. Father had insisted he start work as a hawker at age fourteen. He'd learned typesetting at seventeen. Then he'd been promoted to junior reporter.

Groomed to take over.

He tugged at the collar of his shirt, suddenly feeling the closeness of the walls, the strangling sensation of expectation that permeated every surface inside this building.

Marry well. Run the newspaper. Take care of the family. *Reggie.*

Be his father.

He ran his hands down his face, struggling for focus.

It was only because he'd taken the morning to see Frank, to see the mare. Being out of his routine has shaken him, reminded him of old dreams. Dead dreams.

The swirl of thoughts in his head wasn't going to produce words on the typewriter before him.

Suddenly, there was a new buzzing in the office. He braced his shoulders, straightening, expecting to find his father looming over him, but it was a boy of maybe ten who ran straight toward him, panting as he drew to a stop just outside Adam's cubicle. Adam recognized him, vaguely. Wasn't this boy the cook's son?

"Your mama needs you," the boy panted. "It's your papa. He's collapsed."

1

Six weeks later - Bear Creek, Wyoming

Breanna White could never resist a dare. Today was no exception as she and her opponent waited on horseback near the train tracks at the edge of town.

She'd been sent to town because Ma wanted new fabric for the little kids, who were outgrowing their duds almost faster than she could sew them. Also at home were Pa and six out of seven of her older, adopted brothers. Breanna'd already bought the fabric and been on the boardwalk, ready to head home, when she'd been talked into this nonsense.

She *could* just go home. Or maybe shop for fabric for a dress for herself, something that would shock Ma completely. She should ignore the gaggle of boys nearby murmuring and laughing like geese clustered just beyond the train platform. On the edge of town,

where the prairie spread out in front of them, there
was less foot traffic, but someone could still see her,
and everyone knew gossip traveled faster than the
breeze around here. And a whole heap of passengers
had just disembarked from the train, probably
doubling the crowd on the platform.

Eighteen is too old for childish stunts. She could hear
her brother Oscar in her head as if he'd just spoken the
words. Or maybe it was Cecilia, one of Oscar's adopted
daughters and Breanna's closest friend, who was now
away at the Normal School studying to be a teacher.

But Breanna didn't wheel her horse and ride away.

She never walked away from a race. Or a wager.
Abe and Dougie and Tommy had talked their friends
into parting with their hard-earned money, and the pot
was up to twenty buckaroos.

Behind her on the platform, the conductor called
for the last passengers to board. It was almost time.

The noise from the crowd on the platform faded
away. The grass smelled sharper beneath the scents
coal and steam.

Beneath her, Buster shifted as if he felt the same
anticipation she did, the same pounding of her heart in
her throat.

The other racer moved, his horse stamping his feet.

She glanced to the side. Tommy was more acquaintance than friend. He'd moved to Bear Creek several
months ago with his mother, who ran a dress shop, and
a passel of younger sisters. He was her age, give or take
a year.

"Anybody asked you to the Founder's Day picnic yet?" Tommy asked.

Snickers broke out from her other side, where Abe and his buddies stood watching and waiting for their race. She ignored them, her heart suddenly fluttering against her breastbone.

Tommy was reasonably handsome. Not as handsome as her father. Someone had broken his nose at least once in the past, and it remained slightly crooked, but the dancing light in his eyes more than made up for that.

There was a hiss as the train's brakes were released, and Breanna knew it was moments from pulling out of the station. She was distracted by Tommy's invitation, but not so much that she'd lost track of the race.

The picnic.

Not one boy in town had ever asked her to go walking with him, much less to an event like the picnic.

You're too much of a tomboy to catch a beau. That was her brother Seb's teasing voice.

She didn't want a beau, did she?

Still, it was nice to be asked. And if she accepted, her brothers might shut up about her future prospects.

Tommy tilted his head, his smile just a hint mysterious.

And her insides got hung up, twisting and coiling. "No one's asked me," she said softly.

He sidled his horse slightly closer, but he was a half-length behind her, which meant she had to crane her neck to keep looking at him. And she didn't look away from his smile, even though she was aware that the train was leaving the station, its rumble getting louder and closer to where they waited near the tracks. There were mere seconds until the whistle—their starting gun—and she was...flirting?

Girls don't race.

She shook away the internal whisper and turned her head more fully toward him.

"Would you—?" he started.

And then two things happened at the same time.

The train whistled.

And Buster bobbed his head, but it was too late. Breanna had been so distracted by Tommy that Dougie had snuck up to her gelding's head and slipped the bridle over his ears.

The sixteen-year-old jumped out of the way.

The bridle hung useless beneath Buster's chin.

And Tommy responded to the whistle by kicking his horse into a gallop, surging past her, his shirt flapping behind him.

It had been a trick. His flirting and almost-invitation had been meant to distract her while his friend handicapped her. Cheaters, the both of them.

Anger surged alongside the excitement of the race, and she nudged the gelding with her legs before she'd really thought it through. The animal responded almost as if he could read her mind.

She would beat that cheating coward, and she would beat the train, too.

The gelding's stride lengthened as she leaned close

over his back. She didn't need reins to control the horse. She'd trained him herself, hadn't she? She and Buster thought as one.

As they gained on Tommy and his horse, which only had a couples of strides on them, the train bore down from behind. It was a quarter mile to the winding creek flanked by scrub brush, and she had to jump the creek to win.

Tommy didn't matter at all. He was less than nothing. She was already drawing even with him. It was the train she had to beat.

A lesser horse would've balked at the train's clatter, the ground shaking beneath their feet. But not Buster.

Each beat of the gelding's hooves was like a drumbeat inside her, her heartbeat matching the rhythm. Buster was the fastest horse in three counties. And he proved it as he outpaced Tommy's horse.

She heard the other boy shout over the roaring of the train.

Picnic. One beat, and her thoughts crashed. She lost focus.

Was she so shallow that she'd been easily distracted by an invitation to a picnic? Not even an invitation. A hint at one.

She didn't need a man in her life. Not one bit.

The train whistled again. At her, and at Tommy, who were probably too close to the tracks for the engineer's liking. Too bad.

She bent closer to Buster's neck and murmured to him, asked for more.

And he delivered. He burst forward with one more surge of speed as the train thundered up beside them.

And there was the creek.

She exhaled as they went flying over it, a trick her brother Oscar had taught her years ago. She was one with her horse. They breathed as one, jumped as one.

And they won. They'd beaten the train by inches, but it counted.

It should've been difficult to direct Buster without reins, but he responded to the minute change in her posture and slowed. When she applied the pressure of one leg, he turned a wide circle, now in a smooth lope that brought her back to the train yard. She let her weight settle in the saddle, and he slowed.

She didn't wait for the horse to come to a complete stop before she kicked one leg over the saddle and slid to the ground. The momentum pushed her toward the knot of boys, and they scattered.

But not quickly enough.

She grabbed hold of Dougie's collar and, even though he was several inches taller than she, she shook him good. "Touch my horse again, and you'll be missing fingers."

His face went pale even as several of the others laughed and jeered. He shoved a wad of crumpled bills into her hand, and she let him push away.

She ignored the rest of them. Twice as much Tommy when he rode back and dismounted, talking in a low voice to the other boys.

Boys. That's what they were. Playing pranks like

little children. Cheating.

What did that make her? She'd been the one unable to walk away from the bet.

She strode back to the gelding and had to pretend her hands weren't trembling as she worked to right his bridle.

Stupid.

She wasn't sure whether she meant the boys or herself. She blew a chunk of hair out of her too-warm face.

"I thought I'd have to do some searching to find you."

She looked up as someone jumped from the train platform.

A man. Unfamiliar. But wait. He was wearing a sharp pair of trousers and a tailored vest. Duds like that cost a pretty penny. He tugged off his bowler hat and held it in his hand.

His blue eyes were sharp and betrayed his interest as his gaze swept over her.

She was instantly conscious of the wrinkles in her split riding skirt, the dust covering her boots, the kerchief askew at her neck, and the way her wind-blown hair was coming out of its braid.

Had she really considered Tommy handsome? He wasn't, not compared to this fine specimen of a man. *This* was handsome.

Who was he?

And then her memories clicked into place. This was someone from a time she didn't want to remember.

Her disastrous trip to Philadelphia. She'd been fifteen and determined to meet her birth family. It hadn't gone well.

She'd been walking through a fancy Philly park with Cecilia when she'd inserted herself into a horse race against him. Though back then, he'd been three years younger and not so... intimidating.

Adam Cartwright.

"That was a fine display of riding." His words were complimentary, but his gaze was so intense that she couldn't hold it. Was he being sincere? *Girls don't race.* Her pride was already in tatters at Tommy's humiliation.

"Thank you." Her mind raced faster than Buster had moments ago. She was aware of the town boys still clustered nearby. Who else was watching from the train platform or one of the storefronts nearby?

Flustered and suddenly hot, she bent and grabbed the brown-wrapped packages for Ma that she'd stashed near the platform. She began to tie them off behind the gelding's saddle. She didn't want Adam Cartwright to know how he was making her feel. She didn't even really know herself.

Her discomfort made her voice cool. "What are you doing here?"

"I came to meet the illustrious White family."

She fumbled and dropped one of the parcels.

He knelt in the dirt in his fancy duds, scooped it up, and offered it to her with a hint of a smile, as if he knew something she didn't.

And that made her temper spark.

ADAM HAD BEEN subject to his mother's matchmaking machinations for long enough to recognize the spark of attraction that Breanna White was too fresh-faced to hide.

With the flush across her cheeks and wisps of blond hair escaping her braid, she was just as pretty as he remembered. Maybe more. Her reaction to him made him want to grin, but he knew that would be a mistake.

"He's remarkable." He nodded to the buckskin as he handed her the package.

He'd been glancing around from the train platform, his writer's nose itching to jot a sketch of the small town with its mix of clapboard and brick storefronts, when he'd seen her on horseback with another young man.

He'd noticed the teen boy sneaking up to her horse. He'd tried to shout a warning but the train whistle blew and cut off his voice.

And she'd been off like a shot.

Riding without the use of the reins was a trick itself. Not many riders would trust a horse without reins at that speed. But then he knew she was remarkable. Even more so than the horse, which didn't actually look like much.

"He is. I trained him myself."

She went back to securing her packages behind the horse's saddle.

Adam was aware of the group of teen boys nearby and the curious looks he was getting. After the threat she'd delivered to the one who'd slipped off her bridle, he saw no competition there. But the question remained: did she have a beau? Or a husband, even?

"Where'd you get him?" Adam asked.

She frowned a little at the knot she was tying. Or maybe at him?

"My brother raises horses. Trains them. From the moment Buster was born, I knew." Buster. Somehow, the name fit.

When he'd met her in Philadelphia, she'd made claims about her horse sense. Apparently, she hadn't exaggerated.

She finished with her knot and put her hands on her hips. "Why are you really here?"

For a moment, his thoughts flitted to Father, to Reggie, who was trapped in darkness. He forced them out on a breath and leaned against the platform, waited until her gaze flitted over him and away again. "I told you. I came for you. I can't seem to forget you."

It was the bald truth. Maybe he shouldn't have said it. Or he should've waited until he had more information.

But with her hair slipping from its braid and her eyes still a little wild from the race, he was more intrigued than ever. Good thing it was his job to dig up information.

"You're not married, are you?" he asked. "Engaged?"

She sent a glance past him to the boys still nearby.

Then her chin came up, and she shook her head slightly. The flush that had been confined to her cheeks now spread down her neck. "I have no wish to return to Philadelphia. None in the least."

Maybe not, but minds could be changed. She was attracted to him. He knew it.

And he wasn't one to back down. Not when it was this important. "Can I call on you tonight?"

She was not unaffected. He could see the shifting thoughts in her eyes. And then her lips spread in an unexpected grin.

"I have seven older brothers. You'd better wait until Sunday service tomorrow, so there'll be witnesses."

She quickly stepped into the saddle and rode away without a goodbye. He was left standing there looking after her.

There was no doubt that his decision to come all this way had been the right one. He'd left Philadelphia with a mission. If she was unattached, he intended to bring Breanna home as his wife.

And he'd brought a secret weapon with him, one he knew she couldn't resist.

He almost started whistling as he made his way around the train platform to climb the steps and retrieve the bag he'd left behind. There had to be a boarding house or maybe even a small hotel in a town this size.

He stopped short of the boardwalk as something she'd said penetrated his skull.

Seven older brothers?

2

When Breanna had issued her invitation— challenge—that Adam attend church services the next morning, she hadn't really thought he'd come. She didn't believe for a minute that he'd traveled over fifteen hundred miles for her.

Why would he? They'd only met once, and that only briefly. In the wake of Tommy's humiliation, she'd shored up her every defense. She wouldn't be embarrassed again.

She wished that when she'd issued the invitation to church, she'd remembered her friend Maribelle's wedding after the service ended. She'd agreed to stand up with Maribelle two weeks ago when her friend had asked her.

As Breanna stood at the front of the church beside her best friend, she couldn't help but be aware of the tall, dark-haired stranger sitting in the back of the sanctuary. He *had* shown up after all. Apparently the

thought of seven brothers wasn't enough to scare
him off.

How did the one-room church compare to the
cathedral he was probably used to? Ma had made the
family tour one with soaring ceilings and stained glass
when they'd visited Philadelphia. Breanna had been in
awe. It was nothing like the tiny Bear Creek wooden
building. Or the people who filled it, dressed in their
country best.

Would Adam think she'd made herself look pretty
for him, in her Sunday dress and with her hair pulled
up in a twist behind her head? She hadn't. She'd done it
for Maribelle. She'd never chosen to pretty herself up
for a man. She'd certainly never willingly wear this
dress, with its itchy collar that felt like it was choking
her.

Mama was staring at her. Had she fidgeted? The
preacher had promised this ceremony would only take
a few minutes, but it felt like she'd been standing up
here for hours.

Because of Adam's eyes on her, not because of her
usual growling stomach that wanted Sunday lunch.

Focus. When she was small, how many times had
Ma had to repeat the admonition? More times than
Breanna could count.

Maribelle was staring into the eyes of her groom, a
shopkeeper from two towns over. Most of Breanna's
other friends had already married. Only Cecilia and
Breanna were left. Emma, Fran's younger sister, who'd

lived on the ranch, had gone back East with her brother Daniel.

One of these days, Cecilia would find a match, and Breanna would be the only unmarried girl left. An old maid.

I came for you. I can't seem to forget you.

Breanna's face heated. He couldn't have meant it. She'd met him for all of fifteen minutes, three years ago. He was rich. She'd been able to tell back then, just by his fancy clothes. And the beautiful horse he'd owned.

She'd bested him in a race. And forgotten she'd even mentioned her hometown.

It was a ridiculous thought, believing he'd come here for her. She'd thought of him and the horse race maybe twice in the years since it had happened.

Someone like him would never—could never—be a match for someone like her. She was rural, he was big city. Her family was secure, big as it was. But he was *rich*. The fact that he'd dressed so he looked like a mail-order-catalog-on-foot proved it.

She would never fit into his high society world. She'd proved that already.

She was jarred from her wandering thoughts when the preacher pronounced Maribelle and her groom husband and wife. Breanna's family and the other townsfolk started filing out of the church building.

She hugged Maribelle and wished her the best and then left her friend with her new husband, because Adam had disappeared along with her family.

•

Outside, the afternoon sunlight seemed harsh. Wagons and horses were moving in the churchyard. Beyond that, the land opened up to prairie. Where had Adam gone?

There. He was talking to Pa, both men standing tall and handsome near the family wagon. Oscar and his brood, minus Cecilia, were loading up in their wagon, and Breanna couldn't help but notice her oldest brother's sharp looks toward the interloper.

Her brother Walt, a ten-year-old who sometimes acted like the grandpa he was named for, sidled up to her. "Who's that talking to Pa?"

Her face flushed, but she didn't answer her little brother.

She was on her way over there—to rescue Adam or to join in, she couldn't say—when someone stepped into her path. Tommy.

The heat in her face went right to her temper. She tamped it down. They were in the churchyard, after all, practically surrounded by her family.

The young man twirled his hat between his hands. "You never answered me yesterday. About the picnic."

Over his shoulder, she could see Pa talking and Adam nodding. What were they saying? She should be over there, not blocked by Tommy.

"I think your joke's run its course, don't you?" She tried to skirt around him, but he snagged her wrist.

She glared at him, and he instantly let go, but he didn't back off.

"I wasn't joking yesterday," he said. "When I asked you."

"Then your intellect isn't as developed as the rest of you," she said tartly. "Do you think I'd want to accompany someone who'd play a trick like that? Dougie could've injured Buster's mouth."

"That wasn't my idea. I wanted to race fair and square."

She shrugged. "Then maybe you should've stood up for yourself."

Tommy looked over his shoulder, right at Adam, before his gaze returned to her. Ah. This wasn't about her. Or if it was, it was only in a *property to be claimed* sort of way. He'd seen Adam speak to her yesterday, and now he was interested because Adam seemed to be.

Stupid boys.

She finally skirted him only to find Pa staring at her, his eyes narrowed. Uh-oh.

She went to him, aware of the family around her. Walt was helping Andrew clamber up into the wagon. Nearby, Matty's infant boy Samuel let out a loud cry. Matty's wife Catherine murmured to calm him.

Breanna reached her father's side. "Yes, Pa?" She didn't look at Adam, not with her face on fire.

"This young man wants to call on you."

Now she did glance at Adam, who wasn't smiling, not really. One corner of his mouth was quirked, as if he knew she was remembering her threat. He'd come anyway. Approached her pa anyway.

"You have any objections to him joining us for the afternoon meal?" Pa asked.

She was aware of both Adam's focused look and of Tommy somewhere behind her. Watching too.

"We don't really know each other." It wasn't an objection, or at least not a strong one.

Adam's steady gaze seemed like a dare. "Isn't that the point?"

It was almost as if he *knew* that she never walked away from a dare. "I have no objection," she told Pa.

And then they were swarmed by her family. Or at least it seemed that way to her.

Oscar and Sarah were the first to approach, Sarah climbing back down from the wagon. Then Matty and Catherine, Edgar and Fran, who had a little one on the way. Davy and Rose hung back with their one-year-old, giving a wave before pointing their wagon toward the homestead. Seb and Walt approached last, Seb's hand on the younger boy's shoulder.

Through it all, Adam stood tall beside her, shaking hands and greeting everyone as if he were a visiting preacher or something. As if he weren't worried at all.

"I'll never remember all their names," he murmured to her as Seb and Walt slowly walked off, Seb to his horse and Walt to climb into the family wagon.

She grinned at him. "They'll give you a hard time if you forget one."

His head tilted slightly toward her, and she realized exactly how close they were standing. Close enough that if he'd wanted to, he could reach out and put his arm around her.

He didn't. But he said, "You look lovely today."

It was on the tip of her tongue to tell him she hadn't gussied herself up for him.

He might've seen the denial on her lip—or maybe not. He took her arm and guided her around the wagon when she would've climbed in with her family, who were still conspicuously waiting.

"I've brought another visitor along with me," Adam said, but she hardly heard him.

"Oh, *you're* lovely," she cooed as she approached the stallion. He was a gorgeous black with white socks and one white splotch along his left flank, at least fifteen hands tall, muscled and elegant. He'd been tied to the hitching rail, but he raised his head at her approach, gazing at her with dark intelligent eyes.

She let him scent her hand first, then gently ran her fingers along the horse's jaw.

"That's the way into her heart for sure," Seb called out just before he wheeled his own horse and galloped out of the yard. He'd better be ready for retribution when she found a spare moment later today.

Adam laughed, coming alongside her to untie the horse's reins. "Don't worry. I came well aware that you might fancy Domino more than me. Would you like to ride him home?" He extended the reins to her, eyes dancing.

She felt as if the ground shifted beneath her feet.

Like a train had rumbled past without making a noise or disturbing a blade of grass. Only she was affected.

And she wasn't sure she wanted to be.

She glanced down, away from the intensity of his eyes. "I'll walk."

He fell into step beside her as the family wagon creaked its way out of the yard and down the rutted trail toward home. He held the reins loosely, and the beautiful stallion trailed them.

"Your family seems kind," Adam said after a moment of awkward silence. "Not at all like you made them out to be."

Just wait. If he was to be subjected to a meal with the entire rowdy crew, he'd soon find out what they were really like.

Walt leaned over the side of the wagon. "Philadelphia is a long ways from here."

"So it is," Adam said easily.

"I went to Philadelphia," Ida chimed in. The six-year-old couldn't bear to be left out of anything, often trailing her older siblings. "I rode the train with Ma and Pa and ever'body, but I don't remember it none."

Breanna couldn't help but recall the anticipation of that train ride and her secret mission. The long hours being confined had stretched endlessly. The disappointment that followed. She never wanted to do it again.

"Did you come all this way to see Breanna?" Ida asked. "How come?"

Breanna caught the glance her parents shared on

the wagon seat, but maybe Adam hadn't. He was looking at her.

"Your sister is special. It didn't take more than a few moments for me to realize just how special."

"Stop saying things like that," Breanna muttered, her face on fire again. It wasn't true. She made an impression, just not one she wanted to make.

Walt was pulling a face as if he'd stepped in a cow patty. "That's a long way to come courtin'."

Adam didn't seem ruffled by her brother's nosiness. "I've been further. I once went to Alaska to report on a sled dog race."

Walt's eyes widened.

Alaska? He'd been that far? If he would've been anyone else than Adam—here for the express purpose of courting her—she'd have immediately asked him about his travels.

"I'm a journalist," Adam explained. "I write for my father's paper, the *Daily Explorer*."

Walt's face scrunched up. "That's lots of writin' and thinkin', isn't it?"

Adam laughed.

"Have you read any of his writings?" Walt asked Breanna now.

"How would I? We barely know each other." The family usually got a month's worth of the daily newspaper from Calvin, the next town over, every four to six weeks when Ma's brother Sam brought them out. But she'd never even picked up a Philadelphia newspaper.

"I stored a paper in my bag," Adam said. "At the boardinghouse. Maybe I'll bring it out to you."

Breanna didn't know what to say. Would she want to see Adam again after today?

Thankfully, Penny broke in to carry the conversation. "So your father is...?"

"The editor-in-chief. And owner. He ran the paper himself until about a month ago, when he collapsed from a heart condition."

Penny murmured condolences.

"I'm sorry," Breanna said, because Adam's smile had completely disappeared, and tiny lines had appeared around his eyes.

He seemed to shake himself out of whatever thoughts had taken him captive. "Thank you. He's made a good recovery, though the doctor recommended he not go back to work. I'm to take over the *Explorer*."

Breanna's stomach swooped low, like the time she'd jumped from the hayloft onto a soft bed of hay below.

Adam's newspaper was in Philadelphia. No matter how flattered she was that he'd approached Pa, and that he wanted to spend time with her, she couldn't forget that he lived hundreds of miles from here. The attraction between them might flare, but he was going back.

And she'd promised herself she never would.

ADAM FELT BREANNA'S WITHDRAWAL, but he wasn't going to hide the truth.

Father needed him. Reggie needed him. Even

Mother needed him, if only so she could distract herself by trying to manage Adam's life.

His family relied on the income from the *Daily Explorer*. They employed sixteen people, who counted on the paper staying in business. And now with Father's medical expenses... Adam had had no choice but to step into the life that had been planned for him.

He'd taken over the editor-in-chief duties at the paper a few weeks past. He'd begged off to go on this trip. He might've hinted to his father that there was a story involved, though he hadn't mentioned that it was his own life story he was trying to write.

He'd left the *Explorer* in the intrepid hands of Father's senior editor, a man who'd been with Father nearly from the beginning. Clarence was waiting for Adam's telegraph with the first article.

Adam would find something to write. Later. When he wasn't busy courting.

He should probably feel guilty about playing fast and loose with the truth, but Father's mortality had made Adam take a hard look at his life.

When push came to shove, he couldn't imagine living in one of Mother's society matches.

Breanna would give him a small taste of freedom and be his solace after long days in the office.

If only he could convince her to return to Philadelphia with him.

They'd left the small town behind and only passed one other house on the otherwise open prairie. In the far distance, a mountain range rose gray and purple on the horizon.

They crested a hill, and a valley opened up, spreading out in a picturesque view. A log cabin that had obviously been modified with rooms added on was front and center. A barn stood off in the distance. Another house sat nestled in a copse of trees to the north, a second one straight west, and another to the south.

"My brother Maxwell lives in town with his wife. They're both doctors."

"Maxwell. That's one fewer I have to remember." His teasing words brought a faint smile to her face, but nothing like the easy grin he'd received when she'd first seen Domino.

"Ricky and his wife Daisy and their baby live up north, near Sheridan. They aren't here today."

Before he could beg her for more hints to the other family members' names, Walt ran up to them. Jonas and Penny's wagon had rolled to a stop halfway between the barn and house, and Walt had been the first one to jump out.

"Can I ride your horse?" the boy asked. "Pretty please?"

Adam couldn't help but smile. He'd felt the very same way when he'd first seen Domino.

"Your sister gets the first ride." It was his ace in the hole to win her over, their shared love of horses.

Breanna shook her head. "Go ahead, Walt. I'd hate for my gelding to get jealous."

Stubborn woman. But he nodded to the boy, who was fairly bouncing with excitement. "Should I—?"

"He's a good rider." Breanna smiled affectionately at her brother.

Adam used his hands as a cradle to boost the boy into the saddle, then adjusted the stirrups so the he could reach.

He watched as Walt walked the horse in a slow circle, then trotted toward the open land that stretched out in front of the house. The boy galloped away with a whoop, clinging to the saddle like he'd been born to it. Like Breanna.

"It's a beautiful animal," Breanna said, her eyes on the horse.

"We do have horses in Pennsylvania."

She smiled, but it was a tight thing. Not real. "If you'll excuse me, I'll make myself useful and help set out the meal."

She gestured to the three long wooden tables and picnic benches on the south side of the house. They were sheltered on one side by the house and on the other by several towering pine trees.

He watched her go. This wasn't as easy as he'd hoped it might be. His memory of the connection between them was on target, but she seemed skittish. And she was right—they didn't really know each other. He couldn't spend more than a few days—maybe a week—out West. He might've left things in Clarence's capable hands, but his father wouldn't be happy with that for long. Father only trusted Adam to run the paper. The few days he had would need to be enough.

Walt rode back into the yard, the stallion's hooves thundering. He dismounted the same way Adam had seen Breanna do yesterday, sliding from the horse's back before it had come to a stop. Walt's feet hit the dirt, and the boy kept going, running up to Adam.

"What a horse, mister! He's faster'n any of ours, except maybe Breanna's Buster." The boy's eyes were alight with excitement, and Adam couldn't help tapping the brim of his hat.

"Do you think I can corral him for the afternoon?" Adam asked.

"Sure enough. I'll get some grain."

Adam walked the stallion to the corral off the barn while Walt raced ahead. He'd unsaddled his horse and put the tack carefully on the corral railing. He was letting the horse loose when two men approached.

One was Seb. He'd remembered the only adult unmarried brother. The other was... Matty? That seemed right. He'd seen the man with his infant son in church.

They weren't smiling.

And Matty had donned a silver star on his chest, which marked him a deputy. Was Adam meant to be intimidated?

"Seems like we need to get to know ya better, stranger," Seb said. "You ever play horseshoes?"

He'd been through the introductions, but perhaps this was what Breanna had really meant when she'd cautioned him about her family. He wasn't scared nor intimidated. Mostly curious as he followed the two men to the shady side of the house, catty-corner to the picnic tables, where two spikes had been driven into the ground several yards apart.

He was making his first toss when Seb asked, "You ever been married?"

His horseshoe sailed past the spike, landing in the dirt well past its intended mark.

"Got any kids?" Matty echoed.

He shot them a look over his shoulder. Both men feigned innocent curiosity, all smiles.

"No." He had to laugh.

But the other men shared a look as they walked across the space to retrieve the horseshoes. "You think this is funny?" Matty asked.

Then Seb, "You appear outta nowhere and want to call on our sister? We don't know you. We're only asking fair questions."

He supposed he couldn't blame them. But he put more concentration into his next throw and didn't let himself be surprised when Seb asked, "You spend a lot of time in saloons? Like to gamble?"

This time, his horseshoe hit the spike and bounced off. "No." He made his answer calm when his ire was kicking up. Trust or no trust, he'd pass their test.

Matty's next throw was well short of the spike.

"Too bad," Adam said. "Better luck next throw."

The other men took it for the challenge it was, and the next three turns were fierce.

Adam rung one horseshoe around the spike and rewarded himself with a look at the tables, where Breanna had just lugged a covered basket to the furthest one. She saw him looking, but when he thought she might raise her hand and wave, she only turned back to return to the house.

When his attention returned to the brothers, they were standing with near-identical stances, arms crossed over their chests and chins stretched out almost belligerently.

"How'd you really meet my sister?" Matty asked.

Adam had nothing to hide. "Just like she said. We crossed paths while she was walking with her... cousin?"

"Niece," Seb said.

Right. Because the family relationships here were complicated.

"In a park," Matty finished skeptically.

"And you came all this way after one little meeting?" Seb again. It was as if they'd rehearsed this little interrogation in advance.

Adam swung a horseshoe in his arm and glanced at the men. "I'd never met anyone like her before. Nor have I since."

Matty's wife approached holding a bundled infant in her arms. Adam hoped that meant this inquisition was over.

She handed off the baby to her husband, who promptly looked at Adam. "You like babies?"

He laughed again, a little disbelieving. "I don't

know." He'd never held one before that he could remember.

The dinner bell rang, saving him from what he was sure would turn into a display of baby-holding skills and probably a critique when he messed it up.

Relieved, he headed toward the tables, where the family was gathering. Breanna was placing another basket on the nearer table. When she looked up and caught his eye, he feared she would leave him to fend for himself. But a push from behind—Walt? Or her mother?—sent her toward him.

Everyone stood with heads bowed and hats off while Jonas blessed the food. Then it was a scramble as everyone took their seats.

He ended up on Breanna's right side, young Ida across from them, with another little dark-haired girl and a woman he thought was named Sarah on her opposite side. Breanna's father sat beside her, murmuring to a fussy toddler.

As the serving dishes were passed, Adam leaned close enough that his shoulder brushed Breanna's. "For a second there, I thought you were going to leave me to the wolves."

BREANNA WAS aware of the sun on her shoulders as she squinted at the man beside her. "I still might."

He quirked a charming smile. "Have pity on me."

Walt bobbled the basket of roll,s but Adam saved it,

taking it from the boy before they could spill to the ground. Overhead, the breeze rustled pine needles.

Adam passed the basket to her. "They are very protective, your brothers."

He had no idea. How many times had she felt suffocated under the watchful eyes of her older brothers?

Even Ma and Pa. *No fighting*, they always said. Even though the boys were allowed to scuffle. *Mind your manners*, they admonished. Even though the boys could get away with being impolite.

He leaned closer so he could speak into her ear. "Forgive me for being impertinent, but did your father have a first wife? Each of your brothers is very different from the other."

She looked around at the noisy group. She'd grown so used to it. They were her family, after all. And everyone in Bear Creek knew them. She'd forgotten how her family could present itself to outsiders.

"We're all adopted. All seven of the older boys. And me."

"All of you?"

She nodded and didn't even miss a beat as she smiled. "All eight of us." It didn't even hurt to say it.

"Breanna, could you hold him for a moment?"

Not Catherine too. But her newest sister-in-law passed the baby to Breanna before disappearing inside the house with her husband. Hopefully only for a moment.

Breanna snugged the baby in the crook of her arm, gazing down on the little face with its wrinkled nose. It sure seemed every one of the females around her were conspiring to match her with the Easterner.

Every time Breanna had passed inside to grab a serving dish and set up the tables, Ma had been aflutter in the kitchen. Vacillating between *why hadn't Breanna told her sooner that they'd have a guest* and *he's so handsome* and *what if our fare is too simple for him?*

Breanna thought that if the roast and potatoes was beneath him, she'd rather find out now. Her culinary skills were on the same level as her mother's, passable but not accustomed to fixing anything fancy.

With Breanna's arms filled with baby Nancy, Adam was left to fill his own plate. Judging by the mounds of potatoes and slab of meat, her mother's worries were for naught. And while she'd been looking down at the baby, he'd begun filling her plate too.

She raised one brow at him. He winked and offered her a bowl of creamed spinach.

Before she could decline, Ida spoke from across the table. "Breanna don't like spinach."

Her face heated even though Adam passed the bowl to her pa without a teasing comment.

And then Velma decided to chime in from next to Ida. "She don't much like bein' bossed around neither. You a bossy sort?"

Sarah leaned over to speak quietly to Velma as chuckles spread up and down at the table. Even Pa seemed to be stifling a smile.

Adam took it in stride. "I don't think I'm a bossy sort." He winked at Breanna again.

"D'you play checkers?" asked Ida. "Breanna's the cat's whiskers at that."

Goodness gracious. Even the little girls wanted to make her shine for Adam.

"It's been a while since I've had occasion to play," Adam said. "Although, I did once play poker with a man who claimed to have played against Billy the Kid. I could never verify his account, so I'm sad to say he didn't make it into the paper." He winked at Breanna, but something rang hollow in his story. Was it that he seemed to be showing off for her family? Or something else? She didn't think he was lying. What was bothering her?

The serving bowls had finally made their way around the table, and everyone dug in. Breanna hoped that her family might be distracted by the food in front of them, but it was not to be.

"What does a newspaperman do?" Sarah asked.

Adam was polite enough to finish chewing what he'd put in his mouth before he tried to speak. He told the table about hawking papers and then spending hours every day setting letters in line to spell every word in a newsprint sheet.

"That sounds boring," Walt chimed in from the corner of the table behind them. Was everyone eavesdropping?

But Breanna couldn't help but concur with her younger brother. Sitting in an office all day? What could be worse than being confined by walls and overheated by stuffy machinery? Ugh.

"I don't know about that," Adam said, not losing his easygoing manner. "I can travel anywhere I like—anywhere in the world—through those 'boring' words. Stories can transport me to the Orient or London or even here, the wilderness of Wyoming. And recently I've been the one writing those stories."

Somehow, he made the boring sound exciting.

He leaned back so that he was speaking directly to Walt. In doing so, his knee brushed against her skirts.

He didn't seem to notice, but she felt the touch zing through all her layers and travel up her spine.

"I stopped to stretch my legs at a station in Chicago," Adam said, "and I picked up a copy of a local newspaper. Do you know what I discovered? There's to be a cowboy race in just a few days. Riders will travel on horseback from a little town called Sioux City, Iowa, to Chicago in a week's time for a five-hundred-dollar purse."

"That sounds like something Breanna'd do!" Walt's innocent exclamation sent a hush over both tables. Only baby Andrew's babbling and the scrape of a fork broke the sudden silence.

Someone coughed. It was as if no one wanted to even breathe about her past exploits.

"What?" Walt asked, confusion obvious in his expression.

Breanna laughed, but it felt forced. "Adam already knows I like to ride fast." From the table behind her, she could feel Ma's stare boring into her. She wouldn't give details now, but she could bet she'd be pressed for them later. *Oh, Walt.*

"A race like that would be incredibly dangerous for a woman alone," Sarah murmured. She wasn't looking directly at Breanna, but she felt the words like the dart that they were.

In the ensuing silence, Ma got up from the table and came to Breanna's side. "I've already finished. Let me take this little one."

Breanna gave him up, but her stomach had knotted, and she wasn't sure she could eat the food still cooling on her plate.

"Are you gonna race your horse in that cowboy race?" Ida asked Adam, too innocent to understand the silent tension in the adults at the table.

Adam shook his head. "I wouldn't want to injure my horse. A race like that would be dangerous. You know, I have a friend back home who raises racing horses." His words seemed to be directed to Breanna, though she couldn't look up from her plate.

Girls don't race.

Adam continued, "He has a lovely filly that he's sure will win the Preakness next season. That's a race for three-year-olds," he explained to the young girls. "It's been several weeks, but I got to watch his jockey exercise her. She was a beauty, flying around the track as if she had wings instead of hooves."

He spun the story so well that it made Breanna want to read some of the articles he'd written. He had a natural way with words—and with the girls, who hung on every one. He was naturally charming in a way most men could never pull off. Or at least none of her brothers.

Did he even realize how his voice lilted when he spoke of the horse? He had a lot of interest in it, considering it belonged to his friend.

Thankfully, Sarah turned the conversation to Cecilia and her studies, and the attention was diverted from Breanna.

For the first time since she'd sat down, she felt free to take a breath and eat.

Until Adam pressed his knee against hers beneath the table.

His interest in her didn't seem to have diminished in the face of her family's silent censure.

Her entire life she'd been told she was too much of a tomboy, that she'd never attract a husband.

She'd never considered that someone might like her just the way she was.

It was enlightening. And scary enough to foil her appetite again.

And then Catherine and Matty came out of the house, both holding steaming pie plates. "Who wants cobbler?"

"Breanna made it."

They were still doing their best to match her off.

3

The afternoon was waning when Adam stood from the checkerboard and stretched. "Walk with me for a bit?"

Breanna glanced around them as if realizing for the first time they were alone. Earlier, her father had gone off to check a horse in the barn, and her mother was in the kitchen helping the little ones find a bite to eat.

While lunch had been a chaotic affair, the other families had slowly excused themselves to their own homes, Seb to the bunkhouse, which had left only Jonas and Penny, their three younger children, and Breanna.

Walt had challenged him to a game of checkers that had turned into two and then three as Breanna played dolls on the floor with Ida. The younger boy had grown frustrated at how often he'd had to call Adam's attention back to the game, but Adam couldn't help the way his gaze strayed to the beauty on the floor.

And then Penny had come and claimed the smaller children, sending Walt out to the bunkhouse and the smallest two to their bedroom for naps.

Which had left him alone with Breanna, or nearly so. She'd joined him at the checkerboard and beaten him soundly twice, but he'd made a terrific comeback in the third game and won by a single checker.

She considered him now. "I'll change into my boots."

The sun was setting as they crossed the yard toward the nearest open field. He should probably consider riding back to town, but he wasn't ready to leave her yet. During the course of the afternoon, they'd both shared about their childhoods. He'd loved hearing about her time on the homestead. Chores and riding and fishing and growing up in the country. He'd told her about Frank and their blood oath and his favorite childhood haunts back home. Everything except for Reggie. It hadn't been the right time to mention his brother.

Perhaps she'd sensed he was holding back, and that's why she'd put so much distance between them now. He wanted her closer.

"I think I am nearly able to name most of your family now. Is Walt named after your great-grandfather?"

Her gaze grew wistful. "Yes. Poppy died when I was nine. He was the kindest old man I've ever met. I thought that even before Pa and Ma married."

He must have looked perplexed because she went on, "He was Ma's grandfather."

What an unusual family she'd grown up in. All those adopted siblings, being raised by a woman who wasn't her mother. So different from his own upbringing.

The nostalgia she'd shared filled him with memories too. "I remember spending long summer days with my grandmother. She would sometimes take me downtown to get an ice. She died when I was five." He'd forgotten those moments, forgotten the warmth and affection he'd received from Grandmother.

He let the silence grow between them, entranced by the fiery colors blending across the sky. On the horizon, low-lying clouds turned a kaleidoscope of colors. It reminded him of the Northern Lights he'd been privileged to see during his Alaskan trip. Photographs couldn't capture the majesty of the sunset. He couldn't come close to describing it in writing.

And it certainly wasn't something to be seen in Philadelphia. Had he even made a practice of looking up at the sky over the past few years? Or was it being here, with Breanna, that made him so aware of the beauty surrounding him?

"Our fathers aren't so different, I think," he said when the silence had stretched a beat too long.

She sputtered a disbelieving laugh. "You must be joking."

"Why must I?" He gestured to the land around them. "It must've taken years of toil to build all of this. The acreage, the cattle and horses, hay to feed them all.

All so your family can live in comfort." Even the vegetable garden was massive, stretching out behind the house.

His father had built on what Grandfather had started, but the principle was the same. So what if his life in Philadelphia cost more in dollars and cents than Breanna's life here? They both cost hard work and dedication.

She was shaking her head slightly. Still distant, still reserved. What could he say to draw her closer?

She wrapped her arms around her midsection like a shield. "I suppose you think you know me after today. My family has been doing their best to make me look domesticated. I'm not."

He laughed, because he still couldn't forget that fifteen-year-old girl who'd butted in to a cluster of nearly-grown men. *And* challenging him to a race.

"I don't—"

"Breanna!" A call came on the wind from the nearest house, fifty yards away. Had they been spotted by one of Breanna's multitude of brothers?

But it had been a woman's voice calling out.

Breanna's head turned that direction. "That's Fran. Come on, would you?"

He wanted to haggle for a few more moments of privacy, but she was already steps ahead.

They crossed between a line of trees and splashed through a stream as they approached the snug little house. It had glass windows, even all the way out here.

The woman on the step, Fran, was wringing her

hands. "Breanna. I was watching for Edgar and saw you walking out."

The woman was so distracted she didn't even acknowledge him. "Edgar walked over to Oscars to discuss one of the horses. I thought he'd be home by now."

Breanna placed a comforting hand on her sister-in-law's forearm. "What's wrong? What can I do?"

"The kitten got out this morning before church. I thought he'd come back by the time we left or be waiting on the step when we returned home, but he's gone. Emma's kitten is gone."

A fine tension went through Breanna, almost like a rod straightening her spine. "Do you want me to take a look around? I bet he left tracks. He might even be stuck up in a tree, mewling for help down."

"Thank you." The other woman sighed her relief. "I know I shouldn't be so worried, but..."

Breanna nodded. "I don't mind. Do you have a lantern?"

Fran fetched one.

Adam trailed Breanna away from the cabin. She paused, almost as if she'd forgotten he was present. Her eyes were in shadow when she looked up at him. "You can take your leave. It'll be dark well before you reach town."

"You don't think I can help?" He'd never tracked a kitten before, never tracked any kind of animal. He doubted his skills locating informants would be terribly helpful just now.

Her chin jutted out stubbornly. "I think you're looking for something you won't find here."

"The kitten, or you?"

She glared at him.

"I finish what I start," he told her. Every article. Every frustrating typeset page. He wasn't a quitter. "There's something between us," he pressed. "I think we'd knock along together just fine."

BREANNA WANTED to throw up her hands. The man was as long-headed as a mule.

She didn't want to admit how flustered she'd been by his intent looks all day.

Now, he wouldn't listen and ride back to town. She shouldn't be worried. She wouldn't have to deal with him tomorrow, or the next day, because he'd probably break his neck riding in unfamiliar land in the dark of night. That, or get himself shot if he got lost and trespassed on a neighbor's land.

Obviously, he wasn't going to give in.

He followed her as she walked in slow circles with Edgar and Fran's cabin as a point in the center, slowly widening the search area with each pass. The lantern didn't cast much light, and she strained her eyes to see.

She spotted the first tiny print on the creek bank. When Adam would've spoken, she waved him off. Because when she bent closer, she saw two dark drops on the ground. She reached out and touched one, and her hand came away damp with blood.

Two yards further along, she beside another print and more blood. Bigger spots.

Oh, Emma.

"It's injured," she said quietly. It's what she'd been afraid of the moment Fran had told her the kitten was missing.

Emma was Fran's younger sister and had lived on the homestead with their brother Daniel until a few weeks ago, when Emma and Daniel had left for Denver. Daniel had claimed the bigger city would provide a better life for the both of them, but Breanna smelled something fishy. Both Emma and Daniel had seemed content on the ranch. Their abrupt departure was strange.

Fran had been folded into the family from the moment she'd married Edgar—under duress—but since her siblings had left, she'd been morose. She'd been caring for Emma's kitten, and Breanna had heard her say more than once that Emma would be glad of it when she came back to Bear Creek.

And now this.

Adam was silent beside her through the next fifteen minutes of tracking. Breanna found the kitten holed up in the end of a hollow log. When she reached for it, it scratched at her weakly. When her hand closed around its middle to pull it free of the log, she felt the warmth of blood. *No.*

It only took seconds under the lantern light to see that the kitten had been attacked by something bigger. Maybe a possum. It's stomach had been ripped open by sharp claws. Its fur was soaked with blood, and its breaths were shallow. It was near death.

She cradled it close in her lap, heedless of her best dress. She cupped its tiny head in her palm.

Adam was balanced on the balls of his feet as if he were ready to run for help. "Can it be saved?"

Twilight was falling around them.

Breanna shook her head. "Even my brother couldn't save her." Maxwell was a brilliant surgeon, but there was too much damage.

And Breanna couldn't bear to leave the animal suffering like it was.

"There's a lean-to behind my brother's house. There should be a spade inside. Would you get it? And a burlap sack. Here, take the lantern."

He hesitated then walked off, the lantern's light bobbing until it disappeared through the trees. Fran had left the light shining from the house windows, so Breanna could be reasonably sure he wouldn't get lost trying to find it.

She bent her head over the kitten, tears squeezing from closed eyes.

By the time he returned, she'd shown mercy to the animal. The kitten was suffering no longer.

She wiped her cheek with her shoulder.

"Is it—?" Adam started.

"Gone."

She took the burlap sack from him and gently wrapped the kitten inside and then accepted his help to get to her feet.

She'd been running all over this land since she was a toddler and knew there was a pretty little spot nearby where the kitten could be buried. "This way."

He followed her to a spot just back from the creek bank where two saplings had leaned together, their branches tangling and then growing in what was almost a perfect arch. The ground would be soft here. It almost formed a little chapel, or so her childish dreams had always imagined. It was perfect for their needs.

When she reached for the spade, he said, "I'll do it."

They buried the kitten together. After he'd tamped down the last swath of dirt, she blew out the lantern. Darkness enveloped them, and she was glad of it. Without the lantern, maybe she could hide her tears.

ADAM WOULD NEVER FORGET the determined set of Breanna's mouth as she'd held the wrapped kitten in her arms, waiting for him to dig that hole. Or the pale smudge of her face in the near-darkness as she tried to hide from him.

She was silent as they trudged side-by-side through the darkness. She was heartbroken—and trying to hide it. Over a kitten.

She helped him put away the spade, and they rounded the house. When she knocked softly on the door, it was her brother who answered. Edgar was a little older than Adam, but not much.

An angle of light fell from the open door, and

Breanna stepped back slightly, her shoulder bumping into his.

She was stepping out of the light. Adam realized there must be blood on her skirt where she'd held the kitten.

"Emma's kitten was gone when we found it," she said. *Gone.* A soft word for what he'd witnessed tonight. "We buried it in the woods, beneath those two little arching trees."

Edgar glanced between them. Nodded. "Thank you for taking care of it. Fran would've been worried all night."

Something passed between brother and sister before Edgar turned his gaze on Adam. "Isn't it about time you headed back to Bear Creek?"

"He's going," Breanna muttered. "Good night."

Was Adam the only one to hear the weary note in her voice?

He would've said something to her brother, only she turned toward Adam, and the light falling on her face illuminated the tiny lines bracketing her eyes. She tried to glare at him, but the effect was dull, not like the spark she'd shown earlier in the evening.

So he let her take his elbow and pull him away from the small house.

When her fingers flexed and she would've let go, he pressed his elbow into his side, trapping her hand. He'd wanted her closer all night, but not like this.

She was subdued and quiet as they walked back down the hill toward the big house. The moon was coming up, full and massive and orange on the horizon. At least he'd have some light to guide him back to town. Though he didn't want to leave her, not with the sadness wafting off her.

They crossed the yard toward the barn.

"Why didn't you tell him you put the kitten out of its misery?" he asked quietly.

Her head came up, surprise etched in the slight open of her mouth. Of course he'd known. He'd given her privacy because, at the moment, she'd seemed almost fragile.

"It wouldn't have mattered to the outcome," she whispered. "And Fran..." She turned her face away.

He waited for her to say more. Would she trust him with this?

"It was Emma's kitten," was all she said. And then, "I'm fine. It isn't as if I haven't seen death before." She gestured to the land around them.

He couldn't remember which of the little girls was Emma. But he could guess what life as a rancher must be like. There was never a guarantee when raising animals. Sometimes a calf could be stillborn, or wild animals might attack the herd.

But it didn't mean she was immune to hurt. She was hurting now, trying to shut off herself from him.

She'd offered peace to her sister-in-law, but who would comfort her?

He turned her toward him and took her elbows in both of his hands.

"I'm fine," she repeated.

He still didn't believe her.

When she tried to shrug him off, he reeled her a step closer. He wasn't holding her overly tightly. From the stories Seb had spun earlier, he knew she could unman him if she really wanted to get free.

But her breath caught audibly. She was still fighting this thing between them.

"Tonight you saw the real Breanna," she said to his chin. "The one who does what needs doing."

I liked her. The words were on the tip of his tongue. Somehow he knew they were the wrong words.

"I saw you offer your brother's wife compassion," he said instead. "At a cost to you."

She shook her head, and her face was the same pale smudge in the moonlight.

"You don't really know me." Her whispered protest was weak, and maybe he was selfish to press his advantage at this moment. He released one elbow to cup her cheek in his hand.

"I know you've never been kissed."

He lowered his head and brushed his lips against hers.

It had been a guess, but the innocence in her kiss told him he'd guessed right.

He drew back slightly, not wanting to frighten her. Bracing for a punch.

He should've known better. Her eyes were wide with wonder, and he groaned as he took her mouth again.

She tasted like the cobbler they'd enjoyed earlier in the afternoon. Her hands rested against his chest.

He wanted her closer, but he let her go and stepped back. He wouldn't take advantage, especially when she was distraught.

Adam still had to fetch his stallion from the corral and saddle him up, but he didn't think he could take any more of the soft look Breanna was giving him. Better to saddle up alone.

"Can I call again tomorrow?"

Those words did the trick. She wrapped her shawl more tightly around her, backed up a step. "I guess so."

He nodded. "Then I'll see you tomorrow."

4

D*ear Seb,*

T*HINGS HERE ARE FINE. Daniel is working in a family prac-tice. We have settled into a little house. The mountains are lovely.*

I have no plans to return to Bear Creek. You should ask Lottie to the church social.

S*INCERELY,*
Emma Morris

S*EB REREAD THE LETTER.* If you could call two measly paragraphs a letter.

He thought to crumple it and toss it into the brazier

of the stove that kept him warm in the bunkhouse, but instead he tossed it onto his bunk and ran both hands through his hair.

I have no plans to return. That was news to him. When Emma and Daniel had left weeks ago, she'd been distant and polite as she'd hugged him the same way she'd hugged all his brothers and his Ma and Pa. No hint that she'd been thinking about the one incredible kiss they'd shared after he'd asked to go walking with her after the young'uns Christmas play.

There had been no private good-bye.

He'd chalked it up to the fact that she still hadn't been feeling well after battling sickness for nearly two weeks.

He'd been in love with her for years. Nearly since she'd first come to Bear Creek, a shy, fearful little thing who was hiding out with her sister from a lunatic who'd tried to force himself on her. Seb had earned himself a concussion standing watch when an insane man had tried to kidnap Emma and grabbed Fran instead.

Both Seb and Emma had grown up since then. Emma had found herself in the wide open spaces of Wyoming, becoming confident and showing her kind heart. He'd watched it happen, though he'd kept his feelings to himself until this last Christmas.

After what she'd been through, he hadn't wanted to push too hard.

But she'd sought him out, pressed a brown-paper wrapped package into his hand, claimed it was an early

Christmas gift. He'd opened it to find several hand-embroidered hankies. They were too girly for him, with little daisies and the like, but when he'd raised his head to thank her anyway, his real gift had been the soft, steady light in her gorgeous violet eyes.

He'd asked her to go walking a couple nights later. Kissed her behind the schoolhouse. Then held her close and whispered how much he cared about her. She'd dabbed at tears and told him in a tremulous voice that she felt the same.

And now she wasn't coming back?

It didn't make sense.

Take Lottie to the church social.

As if Emma and Lottie were interchangeable. He'd mentioned the event in his letter to Emma, hoping to entice her to return. Obviously, it hadn't worked.

He'd expressed his feelings in that letter. Told her how much he missed her. He hadn't written that he loved her, though he did love her. He'd held out because he'd wanted to tell her in person for the first time. It hadn't been the right time during the stolen moments they'd had together before. He'd wanted to ask her brother Daniel if he could come courting, but she'd said she wanted to spend a little more time together without everyone knowing. She was still shy at times. He didn't argue with her request—he'd thought they had all the time in the world.

And then she'd left.

He didn't get it. They hadn't had much time together before she'd gotten sick, but during their stolen moments and that one long walk home from Sunday service, he'd spun out his dreams. He'd thought she agreed with his plans. Plans to build a cabin in a picturesque grove on Pa's land, raise horses like Oscar. Seb was a simple man with simple needs.

Was that too simple of a life for her? She was an intelligent woman. Daniel was an attorney. For a time, he'd taken over as teacher in the one-room Bear Creek school.

In the beginning, Seb had teased Edgar about having a bookworm for a brother-in-law, but he'd come to know Daniel as smart-as-tacks, even if he could be awkward at times. And Emma had often been found with her nose in a book.

Had Emma gone away because Seb was so different from Daniel? Because he wasn't smart like her brother? He had an eighth-grade education and could read and write well enough. Daniel had finished both upper school and college.

Seb hadn't thought his lack of education mattered to Emma, but he couldn't figure any other reason why she would've left. Not after the declarations they'd made. Not after sharing that kiss.

He'd go after her if he had to. Denver was only a train ride away. He'd never been to a big city, but he wouldn't let that stop him, not if Emma needed him.

Determined, he sat down to pen her another letter. Maybe he hadn't been clear enough about his feelings. If Emma needed to know he loved her, he'd say it straight. He'd win her back.

. . .

"WHO'S IN TROUBLE?" Cecilia's greeting over the tinny telephone line make Breanna chuckle. Then emotion caught in her throat, and she had to blink back tears.

"Me."

She glanced over her shoulder even as she tucked herself further into the downstairs corner of Maxwell's house in town. Her brother and Hattie were getting ready for their day at the clinic. Or maybe house calls. Who knew? The two doctors were kept busy caring for the folks around Bear Creek. She'd hated to barge in on their morning, especially this early, but she knew Cecilia's classes started early in the day, and Breanna hadn't wanted to miss a chance to catch her niece at the boardinghouse where she stayed in Cheyenne. They usually exchanged a letter a week, but what Breanna had to say couldn't wait.

The last thing she needed was her brother eavesdropping and then reporting back to the family. The way everyone had acted yesterday had made it obvious that no real help would come from that quarter. Last night Ma had smiled a knowing smile when Breanna had come in.

Was it so obvious she'd been kissed? Or had Ma been guessing?

"What's happened?" Cecilia's voice came through the line, cool and practical. Just like the woman. Unflappable.

"There's a... man," Breanna whispered.

"What?"

"A man," this time she spoke louder and then tried to press herself further into the corner. Someone was rattling around in the kitchen.

Cecilia laughed. "Breanna! You finally got yourself a beau? Who is it? Tommy Larsen? Or someone from out of town?"

Tommy. Stung, Breanna couldn't believe Cecilia would've guessed him. Would Breanna have settled if Adam hadn't come along?

"Do you remember the morning walk we took in Philadelphia? Just the two of us?"

There was a beat of silence on the other end of the line.

"Breanna, are you in Pennsylvania?" This time, Cecilia sounded rattled.

"I'm in Bear Creek."

Another pause. "I can't imagine what you're going to tell me." There was the sound of voices in the background and then Cecilia's voice was muffled when she spoke to someone else. "Go on to breakfast without me. Yes, I'll be there in a bit." Cecilia's voice was strong again when she said, "All right, tell me everything."

Breanna drew a deep breath. "Do you remember the young man that I"— she glanced toward the kitchen but could only see a shadow moving on the floor —"raced?"

"Vaguely."

"Well, his name is Adam Cartwright, and he came to

Bear Creek to find me. He thinks he's smitten." The words burst out now. "With me!"

Cecilia's voice was warm with humor. "This is your trouble that's so important I'm missing breakfast?"

"He lives in Philadelphia."

Her statement was met with an appropriate amount of silence. "And you don't want to go back there."

"I can't." Cecilia was the only one who knew that had really happened. Breanna had snuck out of their shared hotel room and walked several miles to the swanky neighborhood where her birth grandparents lived. She'd approached the man who must have been her grandfather—only to be rejected outright. He'd threatened to call the authorities if she didn't leave.

She'd been heartbroken. Cecilia understood why she couldn't go back.

"It's a big city," Cecilia said now. "You might never see them."

It would be just her luck for Adam's family to move in the same social circle. What would her grandparents do if they saw her at some fancy party on Adam's arm? It didn't bear thinking about.

"Maybe not, but his family is wealthy. I would never fit in." How many dresses had she ruined over the years because of rough playing or sheer clumsiness? She didn't know which fancy fork to use at a dinner party. And she couldn't possibly be expected to hold her own in society conversation with her eighth-grade education.

"How do you know? You've never met them."

Cecilia's kind, practical words were like a spark on tinder to Breanna's temper. Her niece was playing devil's advocate, not agreeing with Breanna as she'd hoped.

"I've met Adam," she ground out. "He's well-read, well-spoken. We're nothing alike."

She was a novelty to him now, but their lives would never mesh. It was impossible. Her chest ached just thinking about it.

"And he doesn't know about the seizures," Breanna whispered into the phone.

"You haven't had one in almost two years." Cecilia was being practical again. "Why should you tell him?"

When she'd been a child, Breanna had experienced random seizures. Ma and Pa had discovered through corresponding with her birth mother that the seizures would fade away after she'd reached her majority—which had happened earlier this year.

But sometimes she couldn't quite believe they were really gone.

Cecilia was quiet for long moments. "If you've decided against him, why don't you send him away?"

Breanna gulped back the hot emotion in her throat. "I like him," she whispered.

"Then perhaps you should give yourself a chance."

"You're no help at all."

Cecilia laughed.

Breanna returned what turned out to be a soggy laugh.

"Sure I am," Cecilia said. "I happen to think you're

an intelligent, caring woman who will make a great wife."

It was so much the opposite of what she'd been told her entire life that Breanna found herself blinking back tears yet again. What was wrong with her this morning? She never cried.

"I'm glad to at least have heard your voice," Cecilia said.

"I miss you. You'd better get to class."

They rung off, and Breanna stared at the wall, unseeing. The phone call hadn't helped one whit.

She thanked Hattie, who was scrambling eggs in the kitchen, and walked outside to untie her horse.

She hadn't even mounted up yet when the crazy idea rolled through her brain again. It had popped into her consciousness last night when she couldn't sleep.

The Cowboy Race. Adam had mentioned it in passing.

She'd always longed for adventure. Craved it. And until two days ago, a husband hadn't even been a consideration.

It would take her two days to get to Iowa on the train. The race started soon after.

She could win. She knew it. Buster was fast and had enough stamina to make the long rides.

She swung up into the saddle but hesitated when she should've been riding toward home.

Home, where Adam would call on her again today. Discombobulate her and make her believe she could be his wife in Philadelphia. She couldn't.

So why face the man—and her family's expectations —when she could head straight to the train station?

Had she planned it all along? Because this morning before she'd ridden to town, she'd stuffed the roll of cash saved from egg money and the races she'd won from the Bear Creek boys into her saddlebag. It was plenty for a train ticket to Sioux City.

She hadn't told her family. But it would be easy enough to go back inside and let Maxwell know what she was doing. Her Pa might even guess after Adam's news yesterday.

What was the right thing to do?

IT WAS NOON, and the sun was high overhead by the time Adam rode in to the White homestead. His errand had taken him longer than he'd planned.

Jonas and Edgar stood in the yard near the corral when he reined in his horse. One of them had been riding. A horse still in its saddle stood behind them, not yet in the corral. It was sweat-soaked as if it'd been ridden hard.

He was struck again by the fact that Jonas wasn't much older than the sons he'd adopted. What would possess a man to open his home and his heart like Jonas had? It couldn't have been easy, raising so many kids, and likely all of them wounded by the past they'd survived.

Was Breanna wounded as well?

Adam greeted the men with a nod as he swung his

leg over his horse's back. He was careful not to jostle the bundle clutched against his midsection, not after the trouble he'd gone to this morning to find it.

Jonas's frown was a change from yesterday, when Adam had been greeted with congeniality. And Edgar looked downright murderous.

"Breanna's not here," Jonas said.

She wasn't?

Sudden dread knotted Adam's gut. "I haven't seen her."

The men shared a look.

"She went to the cowboy race. In Iowa." Edgar's voice was as hard as the look he was pinning Adam with. Clearly, he thought Adam was to blame for this development.

Iowa.

Adam's heart banged against his sternum. "You sure?"

Edgar nodded, expression unchanging. "She rode into town this morning and made a telephone call at my brother's house. Then she told his wife where she was heading."

She was really gone.

The bundle he was holding wriggled, and then a sharp claw bit the sensitive skin of his stomach. He jumped and pulled the bundle away.

Edgar's suspicion seemed to double. "What you got there?"

He sighed. "A gift. It was meant to be for Breanna. For Emma."

Jonas's frown sharpened when Adam lifted the fold of fabric—what had once been one of his shirts, now shredded from tiny claws—and the kitten's gray head popped into view. The thing let out a meow, but Adam knew better than to ease up from the firm hold he had on it. He'd learned his lesson trying to mount up with it the first time.

"Emma?" There was something in the undertone of Jonas's voice that Adam couldn't read. But he had nothing to hide.

"You'll have to forgive me," Adam said. "There were so many introductions yesterday." He shrugged, feeling sheepish. He couldn't have guessed which one was Edgar's young daughter. "Too many names to keep track of. Breanna was pretty upset last night about Emma's kitten."

Edgar crossed his arms over his chest. "Emma is my wife's younger sister. She's recently moved to Denver with their brother Daniel. Frannie's been missing her something fierce."

Emma wasn't even here, on the homestead? Then Breanna had been upset on Fran's behalf. She'd shown her sensitive heart because she knew what the kitten meant to the other woman.

Jonas considered Adam. "Breanna told you she was upset?"

"No." Of course not. She'd held back. Everything until—

"You the reason she ran off?" Edgar hadn't relented

from his suspicion, though Jonas had seemed to soften just the slightest bit.

Jonas gave his son's shoulder a squeeze. The men exchanged another pointed glance before Edgar grunted.

"Excuse me," Edgar mumbled.

Before the other man could leave, Adam stepped toward him. "If Breanna's gone, then you'd better make this a gift to your wife." He handed off the kitten, shirt and all, and received a grudging, "thanks," in return.

The man strode away, taking his horse with him, which left Adam with Jonas.

"You and Breanna were out walking pretty late last night. Anything happen I should know about?"

"No, sir." That kiss was between him and Breanna. They hadn't done anything wrong, and the last thing he needed was Breanna's father standing in his way. She was doing a fine job of getting in the way herself.

Had Adam pushed for too much, too soon? He remembered the way she'd responded so sweetly. She'd felt something for him. He knew it.

Jonas nodded toward the corral. Adam joined him at the railing. Inside, two half-wild fillies trotted and paced at the opposite end. Jonas seemed content to watch them, or maybe he was just thinking hard.

While Adam was vibrating with tension. "Are you going after her?"

Jonas shook his head. "She's stubborn. If she's set her mind on racing, there'll be no talking her out of it."

A race like that would be dangerous for a woman alone.

"What about the danger?" He was a little surprised to feel the anger throbbing in his chest, just behind the fear. She was putting her family—and him—through a bucketload of worry.

"Breanna can handle herself. She's resourceful. And tough. She's probably armed."

That didn't relieve Adam's worry. She might be all of those things, but she was a woman. Small-boned and petite. She could easily be taken advantage of.

Of course, there was the fact that she was fast, especially on that horse. Likely no one else would catch her when she was horseback. But she'd have to dismount sometimes. That's when she'd be vulnerable.

If Jonas wasn't going after her, it would be at least ten days until she returned. *If* she returned.

Adam couldn't stay and wait. He'd promised Father and Clarence he'd be back within the week. Foolish, he now knew. And short-sighted. He'd been completely arrogant believing she'd instantly fall for his charms.

Time was short.

He knocked his hat back slightly, let his head fall back as he looked up at the wide blue sky.

Should he just go home?

After meeting her properly, after that kiss, *could* he just go home?

Jonas spoke, his tone quiet and measured. "Breanna has always had a tender heart. But she doesn't let just anybody see it."

Adam supposed he should be thankful for that, but it was hard to feel thankful for anything today.

"She was all of five when I married Penny. Until then, I guess I'd let her run a little wild out here on the homestead. Didn't have much choice without a woman around." The older man sighed. "I guess she's still got some of that wildness in her."

Untamed. That was a good word for Breanna. Like the land around them.

"I'm not sure she'd cotton to someone wanting to change her."

"I don't want to change her," Adam was quick to say. It had been true yesterday.

Today... today, he wasn't so sure. The Breanna he'd created in his mind for the past three years wouldn't have run off on him.

Yesterday he'd thought her independent spirit was something to admire.

Was it that spirit that had sent her to Sioux City? Or his kiss?

I don't quit. He'd told her that last night.

And his gut told him that if he didn't go to Iowa, he'd regret it. He'd already traveled nearly fifteen hundred miles to find her.

But his father's voice was echoing in his head as he rode away from the White homestead. Saying that Adam was wasting his time.

5

"I didn't take you for a coward."

Breanna didn't look up from securing her horse's saddlebag, though she couldn't help the way her shoulders tightened.

"I'm not a coward." She spoke softly, not even sure Adam could hear her over the ruckus all around them.

It was a half hour to dawn, still full dark. The early hour hadn't kept anyone away, it seemed. Riders and townsfolk alike had turned out for the starting gun. There were voices in the dark, some shouts, horses blowing. Anticipation was almost tangible in the air.

Upwards of fifty cowboys had entered this endurance race. She'd never raced against so many, not all at once. Some of the men were green, in it for the glory. Even a city slicker from New York was among them, no doubt tempted by the winner's purse. A good chunk of them wouldn't last to the third day.

It was obvious that others, like the grizzled cowboy

with a scar across his cheek who'd spoken to her,
knew what they were in for. Instead of jawing and
cutting up like schoolboys, he was checking his horse's
tack, like she was. Two other men nearby looked
enough like brothers that she believed they must be
related. Or maybe it was the way they were arguing
quietly.

In a crowd like this, only a handful of men made up
her true competition. She'd know them by the end of
the day. All she had to do was stay the course.

She'd hadn't expected Adam to come after her.

The last thing she needed this morning was a
distraction, and he was a big one.

He'd come this far, it was going to take the force of
dynamite to get him to leave.

She secured the last buckle and turned to face him,
bracing for his temper.

It was there, under his skin, the muscle jumping in
his cheek. He was holding it back by sheer force of will.
He looked tired.

She didn't want to care, but she did. Still. "I told you,
I won't return to Philadelphia."

His lips firmed. "Have I asked you to?"

Stung, she gaped at him. They both knew why he'd
come to Wyoming to call on her. If he didn't mean
marriage, then why come at all?

"I have a couple of days left before I have to return
home," he said. "I'd thought to spend that time getting
to know you." He threw up one hand as if to encompass
the riders surrounding them.

"Come home with me," he said. "Back to Bear Creek."

She couldn't help the stubborn jut of her chin. "I want to race. I *am* racing."

He shook his head. Took off the fancy-pants bowler hat and ran one hand through his hair. "Why did I think you'd be reasonable?" He muttered the words as if to himself, but she jerked as if she'd been slapped.

He sounded so very much like her brother Oscar.

"I don't know." Her voice emerged cool, though inside she felt anything but. "I did try to tell you that you don't know me very well at all."

He mashed his hat back on his head. "I know that kiss—" He lowered his voice, glancing around them. Stepped closer. "I know what happened Sunday night scared you. Enough to run up here and claim this race is all for a lark. You can't get scared if you don't feel anything. Like I said, I didn't figure you for a coward."

She turned back to her horse, fingers trembling as she triple-checked Buster's bridle. She ran one hand down the animal's neck, chasing calmness. If she couldn't focus, she'd be out of the race before it started.

"Breanna."

She didn't look at him. Couldn't. "I think we've both said enough."

He made a noise of frustration. His silence didn't last long, though. "If you're going to race, you should ride my Domino."

It was the very last thing she'd expected him to say, and she couldn't help but turn to him.

His expression was closed off, his hands on his hips beneath his jacket. "I freighted him up here. He's built for speed."

She had to swallow hard. What kind of an offer was that? "What's the catch? I have to return him to you in person after the race is over?"

If he smiled at all, it was fleeting. "There's no catch. You said the race is important to you." Skepticism rang in his tone. "If it's so important, you should have a winning horse."

She didn't know whether to be flattered or annoyed. "You've seen Buster race."

"This isn't a sprint."

No, it was a race that would exhaust them both, rider and horse. She'd have to be careful or risk injuring her animal. But she knew Buster, knew every trick, knew when he had more to give and when there was nothing else.

She didn't know Adam's stallion.

"Thank you, but no."

He nodded as if he'd expected her refusal. And then he turned and walked away without even a good-bye.

She should be used to this feeling. She'd frustrated Tommy, refusing his invitation to the picnic. She frequently frustrated her family when she didn't meet their expectations.

Adam had expected her to stay at home like a well-mannered young woman. He had a right to his anger.

But it still hurt to see the way he looked at her now.

On Sunday, Adam's warm gaze had said *I appreciate you, just as you are.*

Now that appreciation was gone.

She steadied herself with a deep breath. So be it.

Well met, Adam. And good-bye.

ADAM FUMED as he strode toward the livery, where he'd secured Domino before he'd gone to find Breanna.

Seeing her again had tied him up in knots. She'd been dressed like a man in trousers and a vest, her hair tucked into a braid down her back. Even dressed like that, there was no mistaking she was a woman. He'd wanted to pull her close. Claim her as his own.

She'd have probably punched him for it.

He shouldn't have come. Not to Wyoming and not here once she'd run away.

He didn't have to be married to run Father's paper. He'd wanted it, wanted something for himself as he learned to navigate being editor-in-chief and running things.

Breanna was frustrating. Independent. An enigma. He'd seen the vulnerability she'd tried to hide when he'd loosed some of his own frustration on her. Called her unreasonable.

She was, but maybe this was his fault. He'd pushed too hard. Scared her. Couldn't keep his hands off her. She might've responded to his kiss, but that didn't mean she'd been ready for it.

I won't return to Philadelphia. He walked Domino out of the stall as his mind replayed her words.

He knew, given enough time, he could change her mind. Philadelphia was a beautiful city. She didn't have to be chained to the house while he was working at the office. She could do whatever she wanted. Join a gardening club. Or a sewing circle. Raise their children. Partner with Frank to raise race horses. All right, so that last one was the only one he could really see her doing. He needed more time to convince her.

The problem was, time was the one thing he didn't have.

He didn't understand her continued refusal. He fancied her. She fancied him. It was that simple.

I won't return to Philadelphia.

It hit him like a lightning strike. She hadn't refused him. Not really. She'd run from him under the guise of joining the race not because of him but because of where he lived.

He'd gone about it all wrong. If she fell in love with him, found him irresistible, it wouldn't matter where they lived.

He admired her. Was maybe on his way to falling in love. He was smitten, that was sure.

And he had to admit to being envious that she had the freedom to ride in the race. If he didn't return home as promised, would Father try to return to the paper? What if there were a way around it...?

Adam considered Domino. Held on to the bridle

with one hand while he stroked the horse's neck. "What do you think, chap? Do you have it in you?"

The horse stamped a front foot on the packed dirt floor.

"I'll take that as a yes."

If Adam entered the race, Breanna would be forced into his company. It could work. He knew his stallion could keep pace with her gelding. He might not have ever done anything like this before, but if he followed her lead, he could keep up.

If his mother found out, she'd kill him.

He was supposed to be back home in three days, but Father would understand chasing a story. But how would he feel to find out that Adam had been chasing a woman?

He'd once explained his hunches to Adam. In business, his father could often tell whether a deal was good or bad just based on a gut feeling.

Adam was having a hunch now. This could work. He would *make* it. He'd have to find someone in the crowd to send Clarence a telegraph outlining his plan. If he sent a wire after each leg of the race, he'd be reporting from the field. And a story like this cowboy race would delight their readership.

He could do it.

And win Breanna's heart, too.

He just wouldn't mention Philadelphia again, at least not anytime soon.

The first rays of sunlight were coming over the horizon as he walked his horse to the tent where one of the cowboys had pointed out the organizer of this whole thing.

"Cuttin' it a little close." The man spit a stream of tobacco in front of Adam's feet. "Starting pistol goes off at dawn."

Adam paid the five dollar entry fee, and the man recorded his name in a leather-bound book. "No more'n two horses per rider." He slapped a piece of paper into Adam's hand. "Here's a map of the route. Check in every night at the marked location. There's been some noise in the papers about us endangerin' the horses, so we'll have a vet'rinarian at the check in every night. Got some bunkhouses lined out for the cowboys. Next leg of the race starts tomorrow at dawn. No check-in on the last leg. Whoever gets to Chicago first wins."

Did that mean riding through the night? Adam didn't have time to find out. Someone was shouting above the noise of the crowd. He stuffed the piece of paper in his pants pocket and moved closer to the starting line. There were probably thirty men between him and Breanna, but there was no help for it. Her buckskin should be easy enough to find after the starting gun went off.

"There's a crowd of reporters," the organizer called after him. "Give 'em a good fast start!"

Domino danced beneath him. Blood rushed through Adam's veins, thundered in his ears.

He was really doing this. Racing. For Breanna.

And for himself. One last adventure.

. . .

THE STARTING gun went off with a blast, and a horse near Breanna reared.

Buster ignored it as she nudged him into a gallop. Men and horses pressed close. Dirt flew into her face, and she was thankful for the handkerchief she'd tied around her nose and mouth. Not only was it keeping her from eating dirt, but it might keep her from being noticed. She wasn't going to hide the fact that she was female, but she didn't need to shout it to the world, either. Her competitors would find out soon enough.

Off Main Street, the lane opened up through a couple of fields and then the open prairie. With the hullabaloo of the start behind her, she slowed Buster from his breakneck speed to a fast trot. Several others did the same, while the bulk of cowboys spurred their horses for more speed.

"Fools," she muttered under her breath. She could only hope that the vet the race organizers had hired was worth his salt and would keep their horses from running again tomorrow, when they'd be exhausted and lame.

And then Breanna caught a flash of familiar black and white. Was that... Adam's stallion?

It was. And the fancy-pants rider on his back? Adam.

What was the fool man doing?

I don't quit. He'd said the words when she was trying to push him away. Maybe he wasn't a quitter, but he was going to kill himself out here.

He must've recognized her, because he reined in

from the breakneck gallop and veered toward her at an angle.

She couldn't help but admire the leashed power in his stallion's every stride. Domino was a magnificent animal. She could be riding him right now.

But she'd grown up with Buster. She'd raised him from a colt and knew what he was capable of. And this race wouldn't be just about the horse. It was going to test the riders in every way.

Which is why she couldn't believe what she was seeing.

"What are you doing out here?" she called out.

He was close enough with just a couple of yards between them that he heard her. But he didn't answer. "I brought a gift to your home," he shouted instead, surprising her. "I was going to tell you what it was, but I've changed my mind, since you weren't there to receive it."

She sputtered a laugh. He was withholding information to punish her?

She should be offended, but she couldn't find it in her. Somehow, he knew curiosity would eat her alive.

"Tell me," he called, "why are we letting everyone outpace us?"

He was speaking conversationally, as if they were at home sitting in the parlor. The wind whipped at her face. She blinked against it, kept her eyes on the ground in front of her horse. She knew Adam was doing the same, even if he was conversing with her.

"Not everyone," she called, and that was the truth.

There were maybe a dozen riders who had pulled back from the main herd and were now spread out around them. The rest were pushing hard and pulling even farther ahead. Soon she'd be able to take off the bandana that was keeping her from eating dust.

"Their horses won't be able to sustain that pace," she called to Adam. "Some will drop out today, the rest tomorrow or the next day." She gave the idiot racers three days maximum before they ruined their horses.

It was a pity. The animals didn't deserve their owners' stupidity.

All Breanna needed to do was reach the race checkpoint each day before it closed. Being first to the checkpoint served no real purpose. She needed to keep Buster as fresh as possible for the last thirty-six hours of the race, where there would be no checkpoint. Only an overnight race to the finish in Chicago. That last leg was the most important, though each day she must make the check-in to be eligible.

Now was the time to evaluate her real competition, but she found herself distracted by Adam.

She pulled away from him, taking a moment to count horses. Twelve, not including Adam and his stallion.

She was catching stares, either because they thought she was a young pup or because they'd discovered she was a woman. The man with the scar on his cheek was hanging back, just behind and off her right side. Half the time she looked at him, she caught a stare that sent prickles of unease skittering up her spine. She would keep tabs on that one at all times.

The two brothers were there, too, out to the north and slightly ahead.

It was only a matter of moments before Adam caught up with her again, closer this time. As if he'd caught a whiff of the menace in the air between old scar-face and her.

It rankled. "I don't need a minder," she called. "Or a protector."

"Your father assured me of that. I would never consider myself such."

His words might be flirtatious, but she knew he was lying. Why join the race unless he believed she needed looking after?

She shook her head, disappointed. The turn of her head meant she caught sight of his fancy duds, his dark coat whipping in the wind. It was a reminder of what he came from.

And that he wouldn't last.

"You ever spend a twelve-hour day in the saddle?" She already knew the answer. Adam worked in an office, not on a horse's back. "I bet you don't last the day."

His mouth firmed in determination. She'd seen that look plenty of times. Recognized it. Her opponents had worn it often enough.

Not that their determination had helped them.

"And what boon do I win when I ride in to the checkpoint at your side tonight?"

He was so sure of himself, it made her grin, even though she hadn't forgiven him for joining the race.

"What prize do you want?"

She didn't know how he did it while riding at the speed they were, but the hot look he sent her conveyed exactly what he wanted. Her.

"I'll claim a kiss," he said, his voice lower this time so that she barely heard him over her gelding's hoofbeats.

Or maybe that was the pounding of her heart.

A flush heated her chest and rose up through her neck into her face. She'd done her level best to forget about his kiss. To keep from thinking about the warmth of his hand cupping her cheek, the roughness of his stubbled chin abrading her smooth one, the wild swirl of delight that she'd felt all the way to her toes.

Thinking about it was pointless. They would never end up together. Weren't a match in any way except the chemistry that sizzled between them.

Better to forget the kiss had even happened.

If only she could.

DEAR EMMA,

I DON'T WANT to take Lottie to the church social. You're the only one I want to be with. We didn't have a lot of time together before you left, but I should've told you anyway. I'm in love with you. I love you so much and I ain't ever going to stop. Tomorrow I'm gonna ask Pa if I can build in *that little grove I showed you. He'll say yes, I know it. And then I'm going to start building our house. You let me know when you're good and ready, and I'll come fetch you home. If Daniel's the one keeping you away, I'll speak to him man to man. Nothing can stand in the way of us being together. Write me back a real letter this time. I miss you.*

Love,
   Seb

EMMA HEARD Daniel's tread across the floor before he hit the squeaky floorboard beside her desk. He placed the letter on top of her desk. She heard the paper rattle, the soft slap as it hit the hardwood.

"One kiss, was it?" her brother asked. "Because he sure makes it sound like there was more."

She wished she could see his face. If she could, she'd know whether his voice was carrying that fine tension because he was angry or because he was worried.

She blushed and turned her face away so he wouldn't see. But she wasn't ashamed. Not of loving Seb. She turned her face back to her brother.

But she couldn't see more than the vague shape of him. She'd never see her brother's dear face again.

And she'd already shed rivers of tears over her fate, so she bravely sucked back the ones that threatened now.

"One kiss," she confirmed to Daniel, doing her best to sound calm and unruffled.

I'm in love with you.

For three years, she would have given almost anything to hear those words from Seb White. And now... now it was too late.

"We both know I'm easy to love," she said to her brother, trying to sound as if she could tease again.

It was a complete lie. There was no joy inside her, nothing but barren, empty darkness.

She stretched her hand over the desk, allowed her fingers to run over the surface until she touched the letter. Seb's dear letter.

She tucked it into her lap. She wouldn't ask Daniel to read it again. Wouldn't have asked him in the first place if she'd known what it contained.

A love letter. The only one she'd ever received.

She hadn't even expected Seb to write back after the short missive she'd dictated to Daniel two weeks ago.

"You are lovable," Daniel said, and she heard the husky tone in his voice. "Even now. You should tell him."

"No, thank you." She tried to keep her own tone crisp, but tears caught at the back of her throat, tears she knew Daniel heard.

She pinched her lips together, straining for normalcy.

She never wanted Seb to see her like this. Blind, thanks to a high fever that had almost taken her life.

She should be thankful to have lived. That's what Seb's older brother Maxwell had said.

Be thankful for being robbed of her sight? She couldn't fathom it.

What could a blind girl offer someone like Seb? She couldn't cook. Couldn't help with chores on the homestead. Couldn't ride.

She would never see his handsome face again. Or the faces of the children she'd dreamed about having in their future.

What use was she?

None. None at all.

She would write to him. Or rather, dictate a letter to Daniel. Because she could no longer write, either. Even what used to be a simple task, writing a letter, was impossible for her.

She would have to tell Seb in frank terms. She could no longer have the life they'd dreamed of together.

And she was never going back to Bear Creek.

6

That evening, Breanna watched Adam move the reins to his right hand and unobtrusively lower his left to his thigh. He flexed his hand several times. It was the only sign of pain he'd given all day, though Breanna knew he had to be hurting. Not one word of complaint. His hand might be numb, or maybe he had blisters inside his glove.

They trotted their horses toward the huge farmhouse and barn near the horizon. If the penciled map she'd received was correct, that was their check-in for the evening.

Which was a blessing, because she was more than ready to stop. She'd taunted Adam about not being used to riding for such a long period, but the truth was that at home, there were very few days she spent twelve hours in the saddle. Maybe once or twice a year. Her workday was split between household chores and working the ranch with the men. Ma was determined she be able to know how to run a household, though Breanna would rather bunk down in the bunkhouse with Seb.

Adam kept pace with her now, just as he had all day. After his initial question about why she held back from the main pack of riders, he hadn't made another comment, at least not about her riding.

They'd alternated between galloping, walking, and trotting their horses, crossing mostly open prairie with its endless waves of grass and wildflowers.

During the hottest hours of the afternoon, they'd crossed a decent-sized stream, one large enough that it rose over her gelding's knees. Breanna had stopped for a quarter hour and kept her gelding standing in the stream as she used her hat to scoop the cool water over his chest and shoulders, cooling him off. Adam had done the same for his stallion, although his bowler hat didn't have quite the same effect.

They'd covered more than forty miles today, and she was weary to the bone. But her work wouldn't be done when she rode into that farmyard. And she was too exhausted to keep agonizing over Adam's motives for entering the race.

Several minutes later, she and Adam rode into the yard, where several cowboys milled around. A few were consulting with a man who must be the vet, while others were knotted in a group, consuming something that smelled delicious even from here. The excitement in their eyes hadn't dimmed one whit. It was clear they were still wired and ready to continue in the morning.

She shook her head silently. Not a bright one among the bunch. Their poor horses.

She and Adam checked in with the race master, who must've ridden in on the railroad, and were instructed meet with the vet first, then turn their horses loose in the corral and collect a hot meal from the ranch cookie.

She dismounted first, acknowledging the ache in her back.

Adam just looked at her, still tall in the saddle.

"You need a hand, pard?" she asked with a grin.

"I'm a little afraid of humiliating myself when my feet hit the ground," he admitted cheerfully. "But you'll notice I won our wager."

A boon if he finished the day. He'd said he would claim a kiss.

She waggled her eyebrows. "I'm thinking it doesn't count if you can't get off the horse. Hurry up, we've still got to cool them out."

He swung his leg over the saddle and she stifled a smile at the groan he couldn't suppress as his feet hit the ground one after the other. She had an inkling that if he hadn't been holding onto the saddle, he would've collapsed to the dirt.

"Adam—"

"I'm fine." He shook his head, reminding her of Oscar anytime he got thrown from a horse. Brushing off her concern—or anyone else's—and stubbornly refusing to admit anything was amiss.

Adam stretched both hands above his head and then bent at the waist to touch his toes.

The least she could do was distract him from his pain. "What was the gift you brought me?"

He glanced at her from upside-down, his eyebrows lifted in a question.

"You mentioned it earlier," she reminded him.

"Ah, yes."

Probably it wasn't appropriate for her to watch the play of his muscles beneath the fabric of his shirt and dark jacket, but she couldn't seem to tear her eyes away.

"I found a shopkeeper who had a cat with a new litter. I had to talk two six-year-olds out of keeping all the kittens for themselves and then sacrificed one of my shirts tying the thing up to get it out to your Pa's place. I gave it to Edgar to gift his wife."

Oh.

What a thoughtful gesture. How long had it taken him, a stranger, to track down a litter of kittens in Bear Creek? And he'd done it because he'd known she was upset. It was almost unbearably sweet.

Adam straightened to his full height.

"All right, oh wise one," he said, "how shall we cool down our beasts of burden?"

She pointed to the water trough, and they let the horses drink until they'd had their fill, though Adam raised his brows when she let them go on drinking after he would've stopped them.

She and Adam checked in briefly with the vet, who did only the most cursory of examinations.

"He didn't even check their legs for founder," she muttered as the man walked away.

Adam followed her as she led Buster by the reins to the open field off the corral. She was gratified to see several of the other riders cooling off their horses as well as twilight fell around them.

"Maybe there'll be another check in the morning," Adam offered.

Maybe. She glanced at him, ready to comment again on the vet's carelessness, but Adam's gait was off enough that she was distracted.

"You're walking like an old grandpa," she said.

He grunted, his critical gaze on Domino. "I feel lucky that I'm moving at all."

"Better to keep moving now and stretch out your muscles a bit," she offered helpfully. "It will be worse in the morning."

He turned that expressive eyebrow on her again. "Thank you very much for that."

"You could always forfeit the race. No one forced you to join."

She spoke in seriousness, but he shook off her comment as if it were so outlandish that it didn't deserve a reply. "I'm sure I'll be fine in the morning."

"You don't look fine now."

He glared at her, but he couldn't quite hide the lines of pain bracketing his mouth.

"Why don't you let me finish with your stallion," she

said, "and you go rustle us up some supper? We can meet back at the corral in a bit."

He glanced at the other cowboys hanging about. "Will you be all right?"

She resisted the urge to roll her eyes and swept back the vest she wore so he could see clearly the revolver holstered at her waist.

"Are you sure *you* can make it to the bunkhouse on your own?"

His eyes narrowed slightly. He handed over the reins and left her to continue walking both horses.

Another quarter hour and Breanna was satisfied that the horses weren't in danger of foundering. She led them by the reins toward the corral.

Night had fallen around her. The rancher, or maybe the race master ,had hung lanterns on a couple of posts so the yard wasn't completely dark. Cowboys had laid out their bedrolls in the grass between the corral and barn. It would be an early morning.

The corral was quiet, the horses too exhausted to be restless. Only a small cluster of cowboys remained near the bunkhouse and the light shining from its open door.

She'd turned the two horses into the corral when two shadows separated from the rest and approached her.

"Hullo, little lady."

It was Scar-face, and he'd found a friend. The other cowboy had stringy long hair flowing from the back of his hat. Both men reeked of stale sweat, though after the long day she probably did too.

Casually, she rested her hand on the butt of her gun.

Scar-face's friend stopped short, but the other man sidled slightly closer. That was okay. Closer target meant he'd be easier to hit.

"No need to get all jumpy. We're just bein' friendly-like. What's a pretty little thing like you doing in a race like this?"

"Same as you," she said evenly. She refused to let him know he unnerved her with his salacious stare. "I'm after the purse."

"Are you really? Or you greasin' the way for your city-slicker beau?"

"He ain't got a chance of winnin'," the blond man said.

Maybe not, but she didn't need either of these roughnecks focusing on her or Adam.

"Maybe you need to pair up," the emphasis on those two words made it clear what he meant by it, "with a winner."

She worked to keep calm, not to show how revolting she found the thought. In her experience, not showing a reaction was the easiest way to make a hooligan like this leave her alone.

"I'll thank you to stay away from me. And my city-slicker friend."

She didn't draw her gun. Neither did she take her hand off it.

She saw the glitter of malice in Scar-face's gaze.

"H—" Whatever he would've said was lost as someone approached out of the darkness.

"Howdy. Everyone get their horses checked over and turned in for the night?" It was an older man she'd never seen before. He could've been her grandad, if she'd had one. But he was dressed like Pa, like a working rancher.

He didn't wait for a response as the two men faded back into the shadows. He took a few steps toward her. "I'm Hugh. This is my spread."

He reached out his hand, and she shook it. It would've been rude not to. Didn't mean she wasn't wary, after the encounter she'd just had.

"Breanna White."

He smiled at her, and there was nothing malicious about it. "I heard a rumor there was a woman rider. My oldest daughter will be riled that her mother wouldn't let her ride."

Breanna let herself relax, let the coat fall back into place. He was a family man.

"I'm afraid my ma is probably having an apoplexy over me bein' in the race," she admitted. *Racing isn't ladylike.* She should've told Ma and Pa straight out that she'd been thinking about it. But of course, they would've tried to stop her.

"My wife is concerned about you sleeping out with the menfolk."

Breanna hadn't given it a thought before now. She'd been camping with her brothers, but fifty rough cowboys...? And she'd have to watch out for Adam.

Scar-face had figured him for a city-slicker. If the riders thought Adam was meager protection, they might rough him up to get to her.

The last thing she needed was to get him beat up on her account.

"If you've got a loft in the barn, I'd be mighty appreciative," she said.

"We can do better than that. Why don't you share a room with my daughter for the night? She's fifteen and will be delighted to make your acquaintance."

As long as it didn't break any race rules, Breanna wouldn't turn down the offer of a bed. Her abused muscles would thank her in the morning.

"I appreciate that. I'll grab some grub and come up to the house momentarily."

She still had to say good-night to Adam. She hadn't forgotten the kiss he wanted to claim.

AT THEIR LAST BREAK, Adam had dug a scrap of paper and the stub of pencil out of his saddlebag and moved it to his pocket. He was glad of it now, because it took him longer than it should've to jot a few measly sentences about the race as he scarfed down the food the ranch cookie handed him.

Something about the day's ride.

The number of riders.

Over forty miles.

I've never been so sore in my life.

That part wouldn't make the cut. He needed to make it sound exciting instead of like torture.

He was too exhausted to really think straight and prayed Clarence would edit and edit well before he printed any of it.

It took another few minutes to find a cowhand who actually worked at the ranch to deliver it to the nearest town in the morning. Adam slipped him two dollars to ensure that it happened.

By the time he'd collected a meal for her, he couldn't say how many minutes it'd been since he'd left Breanna.

It was full dark now. Idiot. He never should've left her.

He was carrying her plate and a tin of water when he met her coming from the corral, an older man beside her.

He glanced between them, but she didn't seem tense or upset.

She immediately reached for the plate. "I'm starving."

He surrendered it to her as the older man nodded and walked off.

"Is everything all right?" He'd imagined all sorts of things happening to her, but she was safe and whole.

"Fine," she mumbled from behind her wrist, her mouth full.

He could already hear snoring from the men camped at the edge of the field closest to the corral. He wasn't looking forward to sleeping in his rucksack where bugs and all sorts of critters could climb inside with him.

"Any advice for avoiding critters while we sleep tonight?"

She shook her head, mouth still full as she chewed. When she'd swallowed, she said, "Check your boots in the morning before you put them on." She grinned. "I thought you were an intrepid journalist. Traveling thousands of miles and all that."

He grimaced, and she laughed, the sound sending a thrill through every exhausted muscle in his body. "Doesn't mean I like sleeping with bugs and snakes."

"You'll certainly have a story to write," she said, now grinning down at her plate.

It would certainly be a story. His last adventure. After this, he'd be trapped in that blasted office for the rest of his life.

"The rancher offered to let me share his daughter's room instead of sleeping out with all the men." There was a shadow in her face when she said it. Something in the way her face turned slightly to the side, as if she were hiding something from him. But what?

"I'm jealous," he said with a grin. "But I also value your safety."

She glanced briefly at the sleeping cowboys. "Nothing here I can't handle," she mumbled into her plate before she scooped another bite into her mouth.

But was it his imagination, or was there a slight tremble in the fingers holding her spoon?   ·

"I won't let anything happen to you," he said.

He didn't imagine the grimace that crossed her expressive face. "I can handle myself—"

"Maybe you don't think I'd be as valuable as one of your brothers in a fight, but I can throw a punch. And I'm not a stranger to firearms." Though he'd never actually killed a living being—animal or otherwise.

She was shaking her head. "I don't want you to fight over me. You'll get hurt."

She didn't think he could protect her. Or himself, for that matter. Bitterness coated his tongue.

She must've seen his reaction because she quickly tried to placate him. "Adam—"

"I am not one of the boys you lead around on apron strings."

She gasped softly. If he had offended her, so be it.

"I'm a man grown," he said. "In the course of chasing stories, I've found myself in some pretty tight places. The most titillating stories never happen in safety during the daytime." He'd had his share of close calls and had even been in a few scuffles.

She opened her mouth to speak, but he held up a hand to stop her. "It's late and we're both weary. It might be best if you save you arguments for tomorrow."

She pursed her lips, but nodded. Then, she surprised him when she bent and set her plate on the ground. "I'll see to your hands before we say good-night."

"I can—"

"Humor me."

He allowed her to take him by the wrist and pull him closer to one of the lanterns. She turned up his palm, and he caught her wince at the broken blisters where his gloves had rubbed him raw throughout the day. It'd made it doubly hard to hold that stub of a pencil.

She took a small tin from her hip pocket and surprised him when she began to massage a salve gently into his broken skin. Her tender ministrations surprised him.

She looked up at him briefly, then back down at his hand. "I wasn't going to argue."

He let his silence speak for him.

She stuck out her tongue, though she remained focused on his hand, then released it and took his other hand to give it the same treatment.

"You may be right that I've treated you like some of the other ... boys ... I've known."

He wasn't like those young pups he'd seen briefly in her hometown. He knew what he wanted.

"How shall I treat you, then?" she asked softly, looking up at him.

He held her gaze. "As myself. Learn who I am." He said the words quickly when he saw her protest in her expression. "And judge me for myself."

She pressed her lips into a line as she released his hand, but he couldn't read her enigmatic expression.

She tucked her tin back into her pocket and then folded her hands in front of her. "I suppose you'll want to collect on your boon now," she whispered, looking at the ground, at the barn behind him, at anything but at him.

He used one hand to tip her face up to his.

"Not tonight."

He'd seen the range of emotions cross her expression this morning when he'd mentioned it on horseback. The remembrance of what they'd shared and a hint of wanting that again. But also, unmistakable fear.

He didn't want her to kiss him in fear. Or because he'd won a bet.

He wanted her to kiss him because she couldn't live without his kiss for a moment longer.

And if that meant earning her trust, completing this entire race, then so be it.

"Double or nothing for finishing the day tomorrow," he said.

And then he let his fingers fall away from her face.

There was only so much temptation a man could take.

7

Adam woke to someone jostling his shoulder. He couldn't help the groan that escaped his lips. Every part of him ached. Tongues of fire danced down his spine.

What in blazes had he done to himself? Where was he?

Cool air bit his cheeks, and the jostle came again.

"Nygh," he mumbled.

"C'mon, greenhorn."

Breanna. It all came to him in a rush. Bear Creek. Iowa. The race.

Pain.

He forced his eyes open. It was still dark, not even a hint of sunlight on the horizon. Breanna was a shadow above him, her hand still pressing into his shoulder.

He struggled to a sitting position, tangled in the bedroll.

Around them, most of the cowboys still slept, though he could see a few shadows moving around.

"Want me to check your boots for critters?" she whispered.

He couldn't see her, but he could well imagine the quirk of her lip as she said the words.

"Ha."

She slapped his back. "I'll round up the horses from the corral. Get movin'."

He was glad for the darkness, glad that she'd left him to fight his way to his feet without a witness. It wasn't pretty.

Her gelding was tacked up by the time he hobbled to the corral. She'd lassoed Domino and was reaching for his saddle thrown over the corral railing when he stopped her.

"I'll do it."

She handed him the rope halter and went to her horse, though he didn't miss the looks she kept shooting him as she adjusted a buckle on her saddle.

"I'm not going to keel over," he said. It took everything in him not to grunt as he hefted the saddle and slid it over the horse's back.

More of the cowboys were stirring now, rolling up their bedrolls in the pre-dawn darkness. Nearby, two younger cowboys he recognized were tacking up, talking in low murmurs.

"Miss Breanna!" A young voice called out. And then a young girl to match the voice came flying toward them.

He held the stallion's halter as the animal snorted and stomped at the small projectile with her skirt flying out behind her.

"Good." The girl panted. "You haven't left yet."

Breanna knelt to the girl's level.

"We had a couple extra biscuits from breakfast, and Mama said I could bring 'em to you if you were still here." The girl was still breathless but now Adam saw that it was more awe than from the girl's sprint.

He looked back at the farmhouse where a teen girl stood on the porch, watching.

Breanna took a bundle in a handkerchief, giving the girl a hug to her shoulders. "Thank you. I had fun chatting with you and your sister last night."

"I wish I could race like you," the girl said.

Breanna squeezed her shoulders. "Get a little bigger first."

When Breanna released her, the girl seemed to notice Adam watching them.

"You don't look so good, mister."

Breanna stifled a laugh. "This is my friend Adam. He's riding in the race, too."

"You got a hitch in your britches, mister?"

This time Breanna couldn't hold in her laugh.

Adam shook his head, returning to his task of saddling up, unable to stop a smile. There was more movement from the cowboys, and he knew it would only be a matter of minutes before the race was on again. Oh, goody.

"I'm afraid Adam didn't realize what a hardship a race like this would be."

"On his backside, you mean?"

The teen from the porch called out, and the young girl took one more look at Breanna. "Good luck today."

She scampered back toward the house as Adam cinched the saddle tight.

"Here." Breanna handed him a biscuit.

He saluted her with it.

"Knees hurting this morning?" she asked.

The younger of the two cowboys saddling up nearby—maybe Breanna's age—glanced over at them.

"Everything hurts," Adam said.

"If you adjust your stirrups, the knee pain'll stop. I'll help."

She waited for him to clamber up into the saddle, which he did with a white-hot burst of pain up his spine and only one yelp that he muffled with his fist.

She squinted up at him from the ground. "All good?"

"Sure," he gasped.

She touched his knee. He might've enjoyed it more if he hadn't been half-blind with pain. "You don't have to prove anything to me," she said quietly. "I'm not your father."

The worst of the pain dissolved as he drew a deep breath. He smiled wryly down at her. "Good guess, but it was my grandmother who always compared Father and me."

"Really?" she reached beneath his leg and loosened a strap.

He looked down on the crown of her head. Her hat was waiting on the horn of her saddle, so he studied the neat part and dark hair that fell to the braid down her back.

"There. Try that one." She ducked beneath his stallion's neck, keeping one hand on the horse so he knew her intention, and moved to Adam's other side to work the other buckle.

He slipped his foot into the stirrup she'd just fixed. "It's not much different."

"Doesn't take much," she said. "It's right now."

"Granny died when I was five. But sometimes she brought up how much like my grandfather my dad was. Is. And sometimes she remarked on how much like my Father I seemed."

Breanna looked up at him, her gaze open and curious. "Are you still trying to best him now?"

He shrugged, the movement loosening sore muscles. "I don't know. I'd like to think I'm my own man."

She patted his knee. "Done." And backed up a step. "Your own man who plans to go into the family business. Interesting."

There was more to it than she knew. He had Reggie to consider.

Before he could respond, she looked at the young cowboy, who had apparently been eavesdropping. He was fiddling with his own stirrup.

"Breanna White." She introduced herself with a nod. "From Wyoming."

"Theo Johnson. I'm from Idaho." The boy glanced behind. "That's my brother, Archie."

"Want some help?" Breanna asked.

The youth mumbled, "Naw."

Breanna shrugged and went to her gelding to mount up.

She sat tall in the saddle, much more prepared for today than he was. Beautiful, with the first rays of sunlight turning the sky into a rainbow behind her.

"Are you ready?" she asked.

Not a lick.

But he gave a nod anyway.

By MIDMORNING, Breanna expected Adam to ask for a break from the saddle, but he didn't. He bore his sore muscles with white-faced stoicism that she couldn't help but admire.

She couldn't forget his words from last night. *Learn who I am—and judge me for myself.*

So far, everything she'd learned about the man made her admire him more.

But that couldn't change things. She was still determined not to go to Philadelphia. She was considering using the five-hundred-dollar prize money to travel. Adam's stories had whetted her appetite for adventure. She'd always wanted to visit California. Ma was going to be disappointed in her, anyways, for turning down someone like Adam. For going on this race. Why shouldn't Ma be disappointed further if Breanna chose to travel on her own?

As the morning wore on, Scar-face and his yellow-haired friend moved in and out of the periphery, making certain she knew they were watching her.

Her revolver was loaded. She'd checked it first thing this morning, before she'd woken Adam. No telling when a ruffian might get the idea to catch her unawares.

She'd overheard a few crude comments during her days in the schoolroom. And she had seven older brothers. Pa couldn't ride herd on them all the time. Men could be crass creatures.

But she'd never before been frightened like this.

Oh, Scar-face and his friend had only made the one vague threat last night. And she supposed it could be innocent, the way each man kept riding just into her field of vision and then out again. But somehow, she knew they meant something sinister.

She would be vigilant. Not allow them to find her alone, not for one second.

She considered telling Adam that the men made her uneasy. Last night, he'd claimed she was treating him like the boys from back home. Maybe she had been yesterday.

She'd been restless last night, though she should've fallen into bed and slept like the dead. Adam's demand that she judge him for himself had irritated like a burr under a saddle.

She could resist the boys from Bear Creek. Maybe

she'd once felt a spark of initial attraction for Tommy, but that was long doused after his part in the prank.

Adam was self-assured. And he had a right to be, if all his stories were true.

And that was dangerous, because she couldn't dismiss Adam easily, like she could Tommy.

But Adam didn't know the truth about her childhood or the reason she'd been adopted. If she told him, perhaps he'd lose interest in her and return to Philadelphia. But there was a part of her, a selfish part, that enjoyed his attentions that didn't want him to know.

And she couldn't figure out why he hadn't kissed her last night. She'd been braced for his kiss, prepared to bear it, ready to try to hold back the crazy rush of emotion she could expect when he held her close.

Only to be left bereft.

Was it a trick? Had he done it so that she'd spend all day wondering why he hadn't, wishing that he had?

She didn't wish that. At least, she didn't think she did. *Double or nothing for tomorrow.* If he finished tonight's ride, she would owe him two boons.

The land they'd passed through all morning was arid and sandy. Her gelding needed water. Finally, she spotted a creek up ahead.

She and Adam had been walking the horses for the last two miles, and now she called out to him, "Let's take a short rest. Let the horses have a break."

He raised a hand to show he'd heard her.

. . .

ADAM HAD NEVER BEEN SO grateful to get off his horse as he was when Breanna called a halt mid-morning.

He'd challenged her to double her bet that he'd make it through the day, but he wasn't so sure that was even possible. His posterior might not survive the next fifteen—or however many—miles they had left.

The stream they'd finally come across was shallow, no deeper than his ankle, but Breanna wasted no time. She took the hat off her head and, just like she'd done yesterday, scooped water to pour over her gelding's neck and chest.

She'd gotten him this far, so he followed her lead and did the same. Domino largely ignored him, content to drink from the stream.

"Have you seen that young cowboy in the last hour?" Breanna asked. "The one who was—"

"Watching you fix my stirrups?" She was talking about the younger Johnson brother. Adam had noticed the kid eavesdropping on them this morning. He didn't begrudge the kid for following them. He'd obviously recognized Breanna was an expert horsewoman. It was a smart strategy.

"I haven't seen him for a while," Adam said. "I was only halfway paying attention."

That kind of remark would've earned him a frown from his father. Halfway paying attention could get a good reporter injured, or worse.

But Adam had needed most of his concentration just to stay on his horse.

Breanna was now examining the horse's skin

around the saddle. Looking for sores. Smart. "He's been following at a distance, coming in and out of sight, but I haven't seen him in the last ninety minutes."

Adam shrugged. "Maybe he took a break, found a place to nap under some shade trees." He eyed an outcropping of rocks not far away. The boy was lean enough to fit under there. A quarter hour of shut-eye sounded like heaven to him.

Breanna shot him a dirty look. "If you need some shut-eye, lash yourself to the saddle."

"You're joking."

She raised her brows at him in a way that said clearly she was not.

"His horse's gait was off," she said. "If his animal went lame or the boy got lost, he could be in trouble."

He felt his brows rise. What was her concern for the young man? "He isn't your responsibility, you know. Let his brother worry about him."

She didn't say anything else for a long moment. She was facing away from him so he only had a side view of her face. Was she disappointed in his reply? "They were arguing this morning," she said finally.

Did it remind her of home, of her own brothers squabbling? Was that why she was arguing with him?

"If you backtrack to check on him, you'll tire your horse and risk missing tonight's check-in."

She tied off a leather thong behind her saddle. Plopped her hat back on her head. And finally turned to him. "If he's injured or lost out here, he could die."

The boy still wasn't her responsibility.

"And if he's hale and unappreciative of your meddling? He didn't want your help this morning," he reminded her.

She shrugged. "I suppose I'll have the satisfaction of knowing I listened to my conscience."

He shook his head. He was not looking forward to the rest of the day in the saddle, and she wanted to tack more hours on to his time?

"He might not be my responsibility, but the race master won't come after him, and his brother's probably too far ahead to notice." She swung up into the saddle. "If my Pa hadn't come along to care for my brothers—or me—well... I hate to think where we might've ended up."

This wasn't the same, not really, but he didn't argue with her. She'd obviously set her mind to finding the boy and ensuring his safety.

He'd wondered how her upbringing had shaped her, and this was a clear answer.

"And if it costs you the race?" he asked quietly.

"Then my conscience will be clear."

She'd claimed to be racing only for the purse, but her character wouldn't allow her to leave the boy behind. It was admirable, but he still didn't want those extra minutes—hours?—in the saddle.

"You should stay here," she said. "Or better yet, keep riding. I'll catch up to you, even if it's at the check-in."

No. It was a visceral reaction from his gut. She might not think him much of a protector, but he wanted to know she was safe. Out here, she was his responsibility, whether she liked it or not.

He swung up into the saddle, holding back a grunt of pain but not his grimace. "I think I'll try having one of those consciences you're speaking of."

She shook her head but wore a small smile. She couldn't be angry that he was accompanying her.

She pushed their pace into a fast trot as they covered the ground they'd already traveled once. He'd thought the almost-barren landscape with its clubs of stubby, sharp-leaved plants beautiful in its own way, but now he was starting to hate it.

"I suppose you have other ways to appease your conscience," she called to him. "Throwing money at charities and orphanages and such?"

He frowned. "My mother is a patron of several charities." For himself, he'd never bothered. He couldn't even say what Mother's charities were.

He'd never considered it himself. Philadelphia was a big city, and there were too many poor. If he gave a nickel to every street urchin he walked past, he'd be broke. It just wasn't possible.

But the pensive look on Breanna's face and the way she went silent told him that maybe his honest answer wasn't good enough for her. What she wanted was a tall order. And maybe he was a selfish man. He rarely considered the needs of others. He'd never had to.

If he meant to win Breanna over, he certainly wasn't showing himself in the best light this morning. He needed to rally. He'd been singularly focused on his pain. If he wanted to win Breanna, he needed his wits about him.

He was a catch. His Mother had often told him so.

He just needed to figure out a way to show Breanna.

SHE'D BEEN RIGHT.

Breanna didn't gloat when they found the Johnson boy's horse riderless with its reins caught in a bramble bush. The mare was lame in one leg.

It took another half hour of searching, but they found the young man at the bottom of a shallow ravine, one leg twisted at an impossible angle.

Adam was already dismounting when she reined in. "I'll climb down and get him." She started to argue and he added, "You're too petite to carry him."

The boy let out a shout when Adam lifted him and another groan when Adam stumbled on some loose gravel on the climb up.

Adam was sweating and the boy was white-faced by the time they reached the lip.

"Good job."

At her words, Adam shot her a look that told her he'd thought she was patronizing him.

"I mean it," she said quietly.

Adam settled the boy on the ground slightly away from the horses. Breanna pressed her canteen into his hands.

His face was sunburned and his eyes were red-rimmed. He shook his head, and she glared at him the way Ma did to her. "Drink." He'd been out in the sun all day and was likely dehydrated.

"What happened?" Adam kneeled at the boy's side.

"I was crossing up here and something spooked my horse. It reared and threw me. I landed wrong and then rolled..."

So he likely had a host of bruises in addition to the broken leg.

"We'd better splint it," she said. "We can lash him to his horse and get him to the nearest town. There's one halfway to the checkpoint."

Adam nodded. "What do you need?"

He was deferring to her? He was smarter than he looked.

It took another half hour to get the boy's leg into a rudimentary splint—Maxwell would've been appalled —and back in the saddle. Adam's mouth had quirked, and he'd shaken his head slightly as he'd helped her secure the boy to his saddle.

She'd mentioned lashing Adam to his saddle so he could nap, but this was serious. The boy needed medical attention.

She tied the mare's reins to her saddle and swung back into it.

Maybe Adam was right. They'd spent two hours finding the boy, and they'd be even farther behind as they stopped in the nearest town to find help. They couldn't move faster than a walk because of his lame horse.

Maybe she'd forfeited the race because of her choice.

And young Johnson hadn't even said thanks, though he'd had to hide tears when he'd said he didn't think anyone would come for him. He'd admitted that he'd been fighting with his brother.

She couldn't count the time spent as a waste, even if she was out of the race. If they hadn't come back for him, the boy might've died trying to get help. It would've been a fight for him to even get out of that ravine.

So she'd choose to be thankful instead.

8

Breanna woke with a start. It was still dark. Men snored throughout the empty dance hall building where they'd bunked down on the floor in their bedrolls.

She and Adam had been the last ones to check in last night—barely beating the cutoff for checking in—and the last ones to find a place to sleep. She was wedged with her back to the wall, Adam's the closest shadow. She'd slept with her knife—sheathed—under the rolled-up shirt she'd used for a pillow.

No one was nearby. What had woken her?

There was movement all around as cowboys tucked away their bedrolls and gathered their hats. She'd found out last night that seven riders had dropped out, not including the injured Hugh Johnson. That meant forty-three riders were left.

She sat up with a start. Even Adam was standing.

His hands were on his hips, and he was looking away from her.

"Why didn't you wake me?" she demanded.

He turned and grinned at her. She raised one hand to find that her hair had escaped the confines of her braid and was rioting around her head.

She quickly used her fingers for a comb and began the plait all over again.

"I thought you could use a few more minutes."

That was... thoughtful. Wrong, but thoughtful.

She squatted and began rolling her bedroll, her movements fast and efficient. She'd pushed her gelding yesterday with extra miles and then extra speed as they'd sought to stay in the race after their rescue.

Today she meant to stretch out the miles as much as possible, allowing her horse—and Adam's—to rest when they could.

"I heard someone mention a hot breakfast," Adam murmured from beside her. He tied a leather thong around his bedroll.

His hair was adorably rumpled and the two—three? —days of stubble covering his jaw made him look almost dangerous.

She rocked back on her heels, realizing all over again how handsome he was.

He glanced up at her and then did a double take, his gaze meeting and holding hers. His eyes smoldered. "What?"

She shook her head, unable to put into words the

swirl in her belly. He could probably see the blush rising in her face.

"Tell me," he said in a low voice that brooked no argument.

Being ordered around like that should've put her back up, but the pleasurable knot in her belly drew tighter.

"Why aren't you already married?" she blurted. Embarrassment flooded her cheeks with fire. "I mean... how old are you, anyway? Most of my friends are already married off."

And now she was babbling. Lovely. She snapped her mouth closed before any more humiliating words could tumble out.

His eyes still held the same intensity as before, but the skin at the corners crinkled. "My mother is determined to pair me off," he admitted. "But there was always something missing for me. Some of the girls she tried to match me with were..."

"Vapid?" she offered. "Boring? Stuffy?" What had he meant to say? She shouldn't have interrupted.

He tweaked her nose. "They couldn't hold a candle to you, that's for sure and certain."

She could only imagine the kind of girl his mother would choose. Someone beautiful with carefully coiffed hair and fancy dresses. The kinds of dresses Breanna's ma had once worn long ago. The kinds of dresses Breanna would be careful not to touch. Her calloused hands were rough on lace and silk.

She could race, but she couldn't compare to the women Adam's mother would want for him.

Breanna meant to press him about his mother's matchmaking, but the cowboys were abandoning their sleeping quarters, and she needed to get moving.

She mashed her hat on her head and stood, tucking her bedroll beneath her arm.

He caught her hand in his, halting her when she would've moved toward the door. He ignored the curious glances some of the other men were shooting them. He stepped closer, still holding her hand.

"All joking aside," he said quietly, "there's something about you that I never could forget."

Forget about knots and bows. Her stomach felt as if she'd gone into freefall, jumping from the barn loft with no haystack to land on.

"It's my sparkling wit." She meant to bring some levity to the moment, but he didn't crack a smile.

"It's everything. Everything about you calls to me in a way no one else does. Even from across the country. Even across the space of time."

They were standing close enough that, if he wanted, he could bend his head and kiss her. For a moment that stretched long, she thought he would.

Her breath was lodged in her chest as she gazed into his eyes.

But then he simply squeezed her hand and let go.

"I'm going to seek out that hot breakfast. And find someone to send a telegraph." He waved a crumpled piece of paper where she could barely make out scribbled words. He must've spent time on it before she'd woken this morning.

She followed him onto the boardwalk, where a sliver of light was already at the horizon. They parted ways, and she surreptitiously glanced around for Scarface. He was nowhere in sight.

But Archie Johnson was waiting for her just outside the livery with his hat between his hands.

"You all right?" she asked.

"Fine. I didn't get to say thank you last night. About my brother." He scratched the back of his neck, and she realized he was blushing. He was as shy as her brother Maxwell.

"You probably should've been watching over him," she said. There was no probably about it, but if the man was thanking her, maybe he was feeling guilty.

He shifted his feet. "I tried to talk him out of entering. He's too young, too inexperienced."

"That kind of argument from my brothers would've prompted me to enter just out of spite," she said.

His eyes widened, and then he laughed a little. "You're probably right. On both counts. I should've used a better argument, and I should've kept watch over him better."

She nodded toward the livery. Hugh was all right. That was enough for now. "I've gotta get saddled up."

Archie clapped his hat on his head. "I was glad you made it to check-in. Well. Sorta glad."

Now it was her turn to laugh.

His cheeks went even more pink. He probably

hadn't meant to admit he'd be glad to have one fewer competitor to face.

"Good luck today," she said.

She met Adam at the cafe and scarfed a quick breakfast before they both headed to the livery.

Adam had already gone inside Domino's stall when she reached Buster's holding pen.

Whatever good spirits she'd felt at Adam's romantic declaration and Johnson's gratitude dissipated like fog under a brisk wind when she moved to saddle her horse.

Her stirrups fell to the ground as she lifted the saddle. Both of them landed with distinct thuds in the dirt at her feet.

She replaced the saddle on the railing and knelt to pick up the stirrups.

Adam glanced at her. "What's wrong?"

She fingered the leather. It had been sliced neatly through. "Someone cut them."

Adam stepped closer. "What?"

She held up the useless pieces of leather to show him.

His eyes narrowed, and his mouth flattened in a line. He glanced around, but no one in their vicinity was watching. He lifted his saddle and checked the straps and stirrups. They were intact.

Breanna glanced around. No one else was having trouble. Nothing was amiss for any other rider.

She'd been the target.

"Who do you think did it?" Adam's voice was low and angry.

She didn't answer. She was fairly certain it had to have been Scar-face or his friend.

"I need to find the race master," she said.

Cowboys on horseback were leaving the livery in droves. She needed to take care of this before the race master got on the train for the next leg.

"Can you stay with the horses?" she asked.

"I'll go with you."

She shook her head. "Stay with the horses. Somebody who would do this"—she held up the stirrup—"wouldn't stop at hurting an animal."

"Or you." He stood with hands on hips like some kind of protector, reminding her of one of her older brothers.

"Adam—"

"I'm going with you."

She didn't want him to. She was going to confront Scar-face if possible, and Adam would lose his temper. She just knew it.

She tried one last time. "We can't race without the horses."

"I'd never forgive myself—"

She grunted in frustration. The man was so hardheaded!

"There are people all around. It's almost daylight."

She threw up her hands when he didn't relent. That'd been two minutes of wasted breath trying to convince him to stay with the horses. It had been like arguing with a stone, and her ire was high.

Minutes later, she'd tracked down the race master, Adam on her heels. Though silver edged the horizon, the boardwalk was mostly empty. No one but race riders in were stirring in town.

"Excuse me."

The race master was alone on the boardwalk and turned at her strident words.

"Someone destroyed my saddle." She held up the cut stirrups.

The man's eyes went wide, and he reached for one. She let him examine it.

He handed it back to her. "Any idea who would've done something like this?"

Her eyes flicked to Adam briefly, then away. Here was another reason she'd have preferred he stay with the horses. "Two men cornered me the first night of the race, after check-in. They... threatened me." She'd thought to soften what had happened as she felt Adam go tense beside her, but she didn't. No use sugarcoating it.

"You got a name for these two men?" The race master's expression was inscrutable.

She shook her head. "I could point them out to you if I saw them. One has a scar here"—she swept her fingers across her cheek. "The other has long, stringy blond hair. Neither one looks like they've bathed in weeks."

The race master smiled thinly. "After a couple of

days in the saddle, none of you riders are all that fresh." He shook his head. "If no one witnessed the destruction and you can't even name the two men who threatened you..." He said the words as if he didn't believe her at all. "Then I'm afraid there's nothing I can do for you."

The sun was coming over the horizon now, and riders began to gallop down the street in twos and threes, hooves beating.

Her heart was flying along with them.

"You forfeiting?" the race master asked.

Dismay and upset tightened her voice. "No. I'm not finished yet." She spun and marched away.

Adam was wound as tight as a spring beside her.

"Why didn't you tell me you were threatened?"

"Because I didn't want *this* to happen. I have enough protective older brothers coddling me."

If anything, he got wound even tighter.

"Because you can handle yourself." His words seemed like chips of ice.

She nodded, ducking into the livery where only a handful of cowboys remained, saddling up.

Shoot. She hadn't wanted to start out today in a rush after pushing her gelding so hard yesterday. Not that she had a choice.

She was aware of Adam steaming behind her as she went to her saddlebags and rifled in the nearest one until she found a handful of quarters and the two straight pins at the very bottom.

Adam was buckling his saddle on the stallion, his

movements jerky. She'd really angered him. Would he abandon the race? Finally leave her behind?

She tucked the stirrups into her waistband and hefted her saddle onto one shoulder.

She was striding past Adam when he whirled from his horse and neatly lifted the saddle from her shoulder.

"Give that back!"

His eyes shot sparks at her—not the good kind like she'd seen in the dance hall this morning. "We aren't finished yet."

She poked him in the gut but the stubborn man didn't give an inch. "I don't have time to fight with you right now."

"Too bad."

The precarious lid on her temper blew open. What had happened this morning wasn't Adam's fault. But his actions now were irritating her, and he was *here* while the men who'd sliced her saddle weren't.

"I'm sorry if I'm not what you imagined for the past three years." She growled the words into his face, her cheeks hot with emotion. "I'm not some simpering miss, and I can protect myself as well as any man. I don't need your help."

He sneered at her. "You sure about that?" He held the saddle out of her reach.

"Give me my saddle, Adam."

He never broke his stare from her face as he shook his head in the negative.

"Adam—" She'd given him enough warning. She braced herself and threw an uppercut into his stomach.

Only he'd guessed her intention and twisted to one side. With the bulky saddle in his arms, he didn't get far enough, and her punch hit him straight in the kidney.

"Ow!"

"Adam!"

He bent over, dropped her saddle to the ground.

She bent beside him, horrified that she'd hurt him. She was reaching for his shoulder when he surprised her by straightening. He grabbed her with one arm around her waist and backed her up two steps until her shoulders hit the wall. He pressed into her with his hip so that she couldn't get enough leverage to kick him. One hand captured her wrist, and her other arm was pinned where he held her.

She struggled against him, but it was no use.

She was trapped.

"Do you see how easily you can be overpowered?" His words were hot on her cheek, his head pressing close against hers. Otherwise she'd have head-butted him.

"You tricked me," she muttered, still trying to twist out from his grip, trying to find some kind of leverage. "I never would've let Scar-face that close to me."

She went limp, but he was expecting that too and braced her so she remained on her feet.

She glared at him. "I trust you. That's the only reason I'm not pulling my knife on you right now." As if she could reach it tucked in her waistband at the small of her back. She was completely vulnerable to him.

He moved his shoulders slightly, so she could see his face. The darkness in his eyes stole her breath.

"You don't trust me," he said.

And then he let her go, shaking his head.

When she reached for her saddle, he didn't block her way. She hefted it to her shoulder again.

But she hesitated. She should've been halfway out the door, but she couldn't make herself move. He stood there, one hands pressing against his side where she'd connected. Staring at her.

"Would it really kill you to ask for help?" he asked quietly.

She was still breathing hard from their scuffle, though he hadn't hurt her physically. She hadn't pulled her punch and guessed his kidney was paining him right now.

What was wrong with her?

Seb and Oscar were right. She was fool enough to drive away any man who dared to care for her.

She blinked back sudden hot emotion that stung her eyes. Raised her chin. "Would you help me carry this saddle?"

ADAM FOLLOWED Breanna down the deserted small-town street as they made a beeline toward the leather goods store. They passed the telegraph office where he'd pressed a dollar bill on the ten-year-old son of the operator before dawn this morning.

They were the only riders left.

He didn't know what she planned to do with the saddle. Trade it in for a different one? Surely it would take too long for the stirrups to be repaired. Did she even have the funds for that?

The storefront was dark and the door locked when they neared.

You should take Domino. The offer stuck in his throat. He couldn't send her to complete the race alone, not knowing that she'd been threatened by two men. She hadn't even told him the details of what had happened. Had they advanced on her? Put their hands on her? Or just wielded words as their weapons? The thought of it opened a black emptiness inside him.

Breanna banged on the door several times, but no one came to answer.

I trust you. She'd hurled the words at him, made the outlandish claim just after she'd told him she wouldn't allow the men close enough to get the jump on her, but as far as he was concerned, if it was two against one, she was in danger. Even with a knife, or her revolver. She was petite. And a woman. It wouldn't take much to overpower her, even if she was a crack shot.

And there was a part of him that had been devastated to realize she was still holding herself aloof, even after days together. Even after they'd worked together to save that kid.

He'd thought they were building something. Even

just in snatches of conversation throughout the day. Learning each other as they cared for their horses.

She didn't trust him at all. He hadn't won her heart. The race master had asked if she would forfeit.

Maybe he should.

He waited for her to give up on rattling the door, to say she had no choice but to wait for the store's proprietor. Would she be able to make the check-in tonight if there was a delay?

He should have known better than to think she'd give in. She glanced up and down the street and then reached into her pocket to remove two... hairpins? She began to pick the lock.

"Breanna!"

She didn't even glance at him. "Stop worrying so much."

In a matter of seconds, the tumblers on the lock gave way with a thunk, and she'd slowly opened the door.

"Hello?" Apparently satisfied that the place was empty, she stepped inside. "C'mon. This won't take but a second."

"I'm sure this is against the law," he muttered, barely stepping inside the doorway. He couldn't find humor or even more than a vague unease in that fact that they were trespassing.

She gave him a cheeky grin as she moved behind the counter quickly, opening drawers and rifling around until she pulled a sheet of leather and then a pair of shears and set them on top of the counter.

Inside the store smelled like new leather. It was swept clean and every shelf was neat. Someone was going to notice they'd been in here.

He glanced out to the boardwalk. The sun was coming up outside. How much longer until the town began coming awake? The young boy had been inside the telegraph office, but what if he came outside?

What if someone noticed them in here and called for the sheriff?

Did a town this small even have a sheriff?

At least if they were in jail, Breanna would have to give up on the race. The thought was only minor comfort. He couldn't imagine what his father would say if he had to wire him from a jail cell.

She made several cuts on the leather and then motioned him to come closer to some kind of contraption mounted to the edge of the counter.

Another turn rifling through the drawers behind the counter, and she set several brass rivets on the counter.

She went about her task with single-minded determination.

He'd come on this journey with the same single-mindedness. A crazy plan to win Breanna.

It seemed she'd also turned that determination on keeping him at arm's length.

He watched her patch both stirrups, secure them to the saddle, then trim the patch carefully so it wouldn't rub against her horse.

She was capable. He'd already known that. She

hadn't really needed him to carry her saddle down here. She'd been humoring him.

But...

The tumblers in his brain connected like the lock on the door. For the first time since he'd realized she was in trouble, his thoughts crystallized.

There had been something pass over her eyes when he'd asked her to ask him for help. Almost as if he'd hurt her in some way. It was the same look she'd worn when he'd called her unreasonable before the start of the race.

Breanna didn't like disappointing him.

He'd seen her at home, seen her hide a reaction to something her mother had said. How often did her family try to fit her into the mold they wanted for her?

Wasn't he trying to do the same thing?

She left several silver quarters on the counter. More than enough to pay for the small piece of leather and the few rivets she'd taken.

When they left, she used her pins to lock the door back as it had been, and then they hurried back to the livery.

Domino snorted in impatience, and Adam had to rein him in as Breanna saddled her gelding and checked and re-checked the stirrups.

I'm not some simpering miss.

His brain was still working. Still clicking around, trying to make a connection that would throw the tumblers again.

He'd asked for her trust. Demanded it. But had he

really given her any reason to trust him? He'd kept himself from her. He'd kept Reggie out of their conversations. He didn't want her to know about his brother not because he was ashamed of him but because he was ashamed of himself, of the part he'd played in Reggie's accident.

He didn't like talking about Reggie. It hurt to think of that day.

If he had to open himself up to Breanna to win her, would it be worth it? Could it do it?

9

Adam had never passed a more miserable day. He'd barely been able to string together the words to describe it. And he'd edited out much of the misery.

His muscles had finally stopped aching. Either that, or he'd become numb to it.

It had drizzled on them for hours upon hours. He was wet through, and now he knew the true meaning of the word *chafe*.

Breanna had been quiet and pensive, not her usual boisterous self. He didn't think she'd smiled once all day.

He hadn't meant to stifle her.

He was chilled to the bone by the time they'd cooled out the horses. They'd stopped for the night in another small town. This one had two liveries, and the cowboys were split between them.

Ten more cowboys had dropped out of the race.

Breanna had been right. Their competition was dwindling.

Now the two of them tucked their horses into stalls right next to each other.

Breanna turned to him, expression drawn. "I'm going to bunk down in here tonight. There's plenty of room in the stall." She exhaled abruptly, almost like a laugh. "Will you... stay with me?"

Sleep on an itchy bed of straw and end up smelling like manure in the morning? "I'll stay."

She smiled at him them, but it was only a shadow of her true Breanna smile.

"Do you really think one of them will try to sabotage you again?"

She shrugged. "I'm more worried about the horses than anything else."

Of course she would be.

The stable master frowned on them when he came to douse the lanterns a bit later. A couple of dollars in his palm greased their way, and he left them in darkness soon after. Breanna in her stall and Adam in his. Each with their saddle blankets to keep them warm.

It took long moments for Adam's eyes to adjust to the darkness. His horse loomed large in the small space. How exactly did Breanna plan to sleep in that stall?

"I'm a little afraid he's going to trample me," Adam said. With only the two of them and the animals, there was no need to raise his voice.

"He knows you're there," came her voice from the

darkness. "You'll be grateful for his warmth before morning."

Would he? He settled into the back corner of the stall with his legs stretched out before him. In other stalls around them, horses moved around and slowly settled until it was quiet.

He'd witnessed how quickly she fell asleep. He wouldn't have much time to say this...

But before he could find the right words, she spoke. "I'm sorry about earlier." She said the words quickly, as if they left a bad taste behind. "For throwing that punch. It wasn't ladylike. Or kind."

He would've forgotten about it except for those moments throughout the day when he'd moved wrong and jarred the bruise. No, there was no forgetting about Breanna.

"I'm fairly certain I deserved it," he said. "And I have a much better idea now of how you were as a little girl with all those older brothers."

There was chagrin in her voice as she admitted, "Ma has been trying to train the violence out of me for years."

"I believe I provoked it." After how he'd manhandled her, he'd probably deserved worse. "I'm sorry, too."

She was silent, leaving him to muddle through an apology without even a breath.

"I've been remiss in sharing the real me with you. I've asked you to trust me when you don't even know me. Not really. Two of your brothers—I don't remember which—were right. We've really only just met. And it isn't fair for me to expect you to be enamored with me after such a short acquaintance, even if I've become smitten with you."

She was silent. Had she fallen asleep as he was pouring out his heart to her, awkward as it was?

But no, she sighed. "You've used that word before. Smitten. What do you mean by it?"

"I like you." *I'm falling in love with you.* Somehow he knew those words would frighten her. "You do the right thing, even at a personal cost. Even when you're breaking the law." Was she smiling as she remembered this morning's adventure? He was. "Someone has told you your independence is something to be ashamed of, but I don't think so. I like that you stand up to me when I'm being self-centered. The women of my acquaintance at home never have." They were willing to defer to him in everything, so much so that he usually found himself bored to tears. Only Breanna challenged him.

There was a long pause and he began to fear he'd said too much.

"I was thinking today that..." She hesitated. It was so unlike her. Breanna, who was usually decisive and unapologetic. "I was thinking I might ask you to stay on at Bear Creek. So that we might get to know each other better."

One part of him crowed in silent happiness. She wanted him to stay. But the other part... "Breanna." He sighed. "You know why I can't stay."

"Your father is ill. Of course, I understand that. But you could come back. In a few weeks."

The hope in her voice was almost worse than the punch she'd delivered earlier.

"It isn't possible. I have to run the paper."

"So you said, but couldn't you hire someone to run it? Or sell the paper altogether. I've seen how much you love the wide open spaces here. And your writing. What if... you could start a paper in Bear Creek?"

He shook his head, expelling a frustrated breath. She didn't understand what she was asking. He did think it was beautiful here. But he was only experiencing his last adventure. He couldn't stay. He had a duty to Reggie.

"It isn't that easy," he finally said. "I can't just abandon the *Explorer*. And starting a new business in an untried area..." He shook his head even though she couldn't see him. "My grandfather and my father spent decades building the paper into what it is now. It is my family's legacy."

"Do you even want it?" she asked quietly. "Because every time you mention it..."

"What?" Every time he mentioned it, *what*?

A beat. "Nothing."

"Don't hold back now," he said, and if his voice was curt, he couldn't help it.

But she said nothing in response.

He exhaled silently. He shouldn't lose his temper with her just because she challenged him. Hadn't he all but asked her to challenge him?

"It doesn't matter whether I want the paper," he said. "It's mine to run."

He rubbed one hand over his face. He hadn't noticed the long hours in the saddle today. Not after the first two painful days. But somehow he knew he would suffer through each hour that dragged past quitting time at the paper, even behind his father's desk.

"Am I really just supposed to be your novelty?" she asked. "To be taken off the shelf when you arrive home late from work? Or to attend parties on your arm, so that all of your friends can admire your unconventional wife? Am I just to sit and wait for you all the time?"

She made it sound awful, when it would be anything but. "You would have as much freedom as you wanted," he told her. "You could come and go as you pleased. Have a stable full of horses to enjoy at your leisure."

"I don't need leisure!" She made an exasperated noise. "I like working the horses. And I don't want to live life by myself because you'll be chained to your desk in the office. You would ask me to give up my entire life for that?"

Bitterness rose in his throat. She was right. Why should she give up her family, her freedom to move across the country for *him*? He was a fool even to have imagined it.

"If you can ask me to give up everything, why should I not do the same?" she asked quietly.

His stomach lurched. What was she saying?

"Come to Wyoming. Make your life there. You could do whatever you wanted. Start a paper. Raise horses. Write a dime novel. We could make a life together. There."

We could make a life together. For a few seconds, the possibility stretched out before him. He could almost see it, taste it. A little cabin of their own. Raising race-horses, both strong and smart. And kids, little towheaded versions of Breanna that ran wild with their cousins.

And what of his father? And Reggie? Should he just abandon them?

He shook away the daydream, allowed himself to see only the darkness around him. "I can't. You know I can't."

BREANNA HAD KNOWN Adam would say no, but for one shining moment, she'd felt his stillness, felt him considering her suggestion.

She tipped her head back against the corner of the stall where she'd curled up with her bedroll. Forced her eyes to close. She needed rest for the race tomorrow. Two more days of difficult terrain and then the twenty-four hour stretch where she'd see what she and her gelding had left. Whether they could beat the remaining competition.

But apparently, Adam didn't consider their conversation finished.

"When I was younger... I don't know. Maybe about ten. I was horse crazy. My brother, too. He was two years younger and followed me everywhere. Father worked all the time, and Reggie and I decided to visit a friend of ours who had a stable full of horses."

Adam's voice was so serious in the darkness. This was the first time he'd mentioned his brother. Why was that?

"It was all in fun," he continued. "We'd ridden before. We saddled up two of our favorites and set off."

Her stomach twisted as his words made her antici-pate something ominous.

"Something spooked his horse and it reared. He was tossed to the ground. He broke his back."

"Oh, Adam," she breathed. She wished they weren't separated by the stall wall. Her hands itched to reach for him, to comfort him.

"It had been my idea to go riding that day. Father blamed me. I blame myself."

"Is he...?"

"Confined to a wheeled chair. He never leaves the house."

A small relief flitted through her. She'd been afraid Adam was going to say his brother had died. But no. Confined to a chair.

It sounded awful to someone like her, someone who cherished her freedom and the ability to ride where the wind took her.

But then, Hattie sometimes found herself confined to a chair when her multiple sclerosis made it impos-sible to stand upright. And she was a doctor! She still practiced, still bore her load of patients even if she didn't perform surgery on bad days.

"And does your brother not want to help in acting as publisher for the paper?" she asked softly.

He was quiet for a long moment. "When I was a child, I dreamed of horses. Reggie was always so serious. I think he dreamed of ink-stained fingers and the paper." There was movement from his side of the stall, as if he'd shifted restlessly. "It's impossible. He doesn't leave the house."

And because of that, neither of them would live their childhood dreams. Life had crushed them both.

It was clear what drove Adam to take over the family legacy, even though she believed he didn't want it. A terrible guilt.

"It wasn't your fault," she said, her voice small in the darkness.

"Of course it was." His bitterness was palpable. "If I'd been a less adamant that we go, or *more* adamant that he stay home..."

He didn't finish his thought, but she could guess his meaning. *Everything would be different now.*

She knew a thing or two about guilt. About unmet family expectations. The mere idea of her as an infant had been so terrifying that her own mother had disposed of her. That left some kind of stain on Breanna's heart, one that would never heal. Three years ago, she'd hoped to find answers, but there were none to be had.

Sometimes, life bucked you off, and there was no way to get back on.

She wouldn't demand Adam stay in Wyoming. But neither could she go back to Philadelphia with him.

Better to put some distance between them now. Even if she'd liked the protective side of him—against her better judgment.

It didn't matter how much she liked the man. Their lives were headed in two different directions.

It would never work.

10

Another drizzly day, and Breanna had been on edge since she'd ridden out at dawn with a subdued Adam.

Maybe she'd said too much last night. He'd spoken hesitatingly of his brother and his father's expectations. It sounded hard. What would Pa do if she announced she was leaving home? Maybe he was even expecting it since Adam had come into her life.

He would give her his blessing. And go with her until she was settled, if she asked.

Adam didn't have that.

She'd gone to sleep determined to put as much distance between them as possible, but she'd woken with a new determination.

Breanna hated to see him so trapped. He hadn't said that his brother was helpless. Only that he never left the house.

What if there was a chance that Adam could make a life in Wyoming? Even a slim chance could be enough.

Because she'd fallen for the man.

She'd come to the realization as they'd saddled up, quiet and efficient in the pre-dawn light.

He'd offered her a hand up into the saddle, and she'd taken it in the name of efficiency.

It was everything. The warmth of his palm against hers. The strength he exuded but didn't make a big deal of. The heavy burden he bore. He cared deeply for his brother, though he hadn't said it in as many words.

And then there was the fact that, after his initial appearance at the race starting line, he hadn't asked her to quit. He was willing to ride beside her.

She'd instantly become flustered and hot, hiding her face beneath her hat brim as she pretended to adjust a buckle at her knee opposite Adam.

She'd barely been able to look at him since.

Her brothers would likely think it outrageously funny. Breanna in love with someone like Adam.

Or maybe they wouldn't. Except Seb, each of her older brothers had found his own happiness.

She didn't know what to do with the newfound knowledge of her feelings. If Adam discovered the truth, he'd press her to go home with him.

Her own plan to convince him to come back after he'd settled things with his father and brother depended on Adam's feelings for her. He didn't need to know she'd gone and fallen for him.

But she wasn't sure she could keep it a secret, not

when every time she looked at him, she could feel it shining like a lamp in the dark.

Her thoughts were jumbled so that she wasn't prepared for the steep, rocky decline that seemed to come upon them in an instant. She reined in at the lip of the depression. She should've studied the map better once it had gotten light enough this morning, though the crude drawing probably didn't have any clues how to traverse this difficult section. They'd passed a couple of other riders during the morning; once they'd seen a pair out in the far distance in front of them.

The land stretched out before them, green and flat, a small town almost at the horizon. And there was a creek down there, which was good. But the rocky hill would be difficult to traverse.

Adam reined in beside her. "Problem?" Steady and unflappable, as always.

"No." She gazed down, trying to see a path that wouldn't lead to her horse breaking a leg.

"There." Adam pointed to what might be a deer track that weaved its way down the hill and through some boulders. It looked safe enough.

"Fine," she agreed.

"Mind if I go first?" he asked. "This old boy is sweating under the sun. I'll give him a few moments in the creek."

Looking at Adam tall in the saddle, she almost felt a need to take her hat off and fan herself with it. Yes, a break was in order.

She watched as Adam descended the hill. With the

loose gravel and untraveled terrain, she'd let him get well down the hill before she started after him. It was safer that way.

She turned to gaze at the land they'd just crossed. Scar-face was coming up behind them, his blond-haired crony nowhere in sight.

The man was at a flat-out gallop and would reach the hill in moments. Breanna could wait until he'd descended to start down, but with Adam so far away, she... yes, she wanted him near, if only for the safety of numbers.

Adam and his stallion were far enough down that it would be safe to start. She'd be more than halfway down by the time Scar-face arrived at the top.

Her gelding was surefooted as they began their descent. The deer track was old and somewhat over-grown in the few places that had enough soil for grass to cling to.

She was peripherally aware of Adam waving to her from the bottom of the hill. He was safe.

But she was only a third of the way down when tiny pieces of gravel began rolling past her, pinging down the hill as they fell.

She spared a quick glance behind to see that Scar-face was coming directly down the hill, not on the deer path. It was dangerous and wouldn't save him that much time.

How had he caught up so quickly? Maybe she'd misjudged his distance.

She brought her focus back to the task. He might be

willing to risk his horse, but she wasn't. Buster shied once as more gravel shifted behind them, rolling into their path. Did the man have a death wish? Or was he trying to intimidate her?

The deer track should put her out of his direct path right about... now. She urged Buster for more speed. She wanted to put more distance between them and the man. And she did, Buster understanding her urgency and responding.

Her relief was short lived as Adam gave an indistinct shout from below.

Scar-face drew up on the hill just above her.

Where had he come from? She was sure his direct path down the hill had been well behind her.

She had no time for questions or to reprimand him for riding so close on a dangerous path. Buster fought for footing as the other horse shifted gravel from above.

She was pulling back on the reins to slow and let Scar-face pass when his horse shifted even closer. Was he slipping, losing his footing—?

But the quick glance she got showed malice in his eyes as he reached out for her.

She thought she caught the wink of sunlight on metal. Had he pulled a knife?

She twisted away, trying to get out of his reach, and it put her off-balance.

Scar-face's shove knocked her out of the saddle.

She'd been taught to always roll into the fall, but

she'd never fallen on a hill like this. She was afraid she'd roll all the way down.

That fear made her flail and reach out. She landed hard on her wrist and shoulder, losing her breath entirely.

She heard Scar-face's horse gallop off, heard the sound of Buster scrabbling for footing.

She couldn't catch her breath.

Adam shouted her name.

But she couldn't answer him.

ADAM HAD ALREADY DISMOUNTED as he waited for Breanna at the bottom of that mountainous hill.

There'd been an awkwardness between them this morning. He'd caught her glance when they'd been first riding out. Thought he read something that gave him great hope.

But she'd been quiet and distant. He was looking forward to the break they'd give the horses.

Maybe it was time to cash in on the boons he'd won.

Adam saw the man—so much taller and more muscular than Breanna—start down the hill. From here, he couldn't see the man's features. Was it the one who'd threatened her before?

Then the man draw his horse right up to her.

Adam shouted a warning. But it was utterly useless.

She tumbled off her horse.

The path was lined with huge boulders and smaller

rocks. If she landed wrong... They were miles from any kind of help. Who even knew if that town he'd seen on the horizon had a doctor?

He started up the hill without thinking that it might've been faster to get back on his horse. Breanna's horse had galloped several paces away and then stopped.

"Breanna!"

She didn't answer, and his past entwined with the present for too many breaths as he struggled up the hill. *Please, don't let her neck be broken. Or her back. Don't let her be bleeding out.*

The rough cowboy galloped past him, sending a scornful glance and rocks skittering. Adam had to fight for his footing but got a glance at the man's scarred cheek and dead eyes.

For a blinding second, Adam thought of jumping toward the man. He could grab his leg, rip him bodily off the horse. Pummel him. Kill him.

But Breanna needed him.

He couldn't bear it if he lost someone else on his watch.

He continued up the slope, gasping for breath. When he finally reached her, he slid to his knees beside her on the rocky ground, barely noticing that he'd ripped the knee of his pants. She was prone, face-down, her hat obscuring her face.

He pulled it away. "Breanna!"

There was no blood. And her lashes were dark against the pale, unblemished cheeks.

She breathed in a quivering breath and then again, more deeply.

She struggled for words, and he bent his head close to hers. "My horse?" came her broken whisper.

Relief rushed through him with a roar. If she were asking about her horse, she couldn't be on death's doorstep. Or maybe she could. This was Breanna, after all.

But beautiful color filled her face, and she was already starting to push off the ground.

"Easy," he said. He put a hand beneath her arm to help her sit upright.

He glanced around. He hadn't even considered the horse in his single-mindedness to get to his woman.

"There." He jerked his chin, not wanting to let go of her now that he'd gotten both hands on her shoulders.

The horse was standing nearby, waiting. A well-trained animal. And it looked fine, not that he was in a rush to check it.

She was still working to steady her breaths.

"What hurts?" He ran both hands down her arms. She flinched slightly when he touched her left wrist. He studied it, but it seemed fine from the outside. No cuts or scrapes.

"Anywhere else?"

She shook her head, but he cupped her jaw with both hands. "You've a scrape, here." He gently rubbed his thumb beneath a raw spot at her jaw.

Her eyes looked luminous, and the breath that had been cinched tight in his chest finally found its relief. It sawed out of him as he leaned his forehead against hers and closed his eyes.

She let him hold her there for a few moments and then cleared her throat.

He let her go. Straightened to his full height and offered her his hand. She took it and stood.

There were a million things he wanted her to know, a million thoughts bouncing in his mind, but words failed him.

"Scared you for a minute?" She touched his forearm. "Me too."

He exhaled roughly again. At least she had some sense of her own mortality.

He didn't answer. It didn't seem necessary after what he'd shared last night. She knew that he'd flashed back to those awful moments when Reggie had fallen from that horse so many years ago.

She paused. "You know, if I *was* hurt, it wouldn't have been your fault."

He was mired in the frozen darkness inside. "That's not what it feels like."

Her gaze was frank and curious. "If you fell, would you blame me?"

He'd chased her out here across the plains. Maybe he could blame her, but of course he wouldn't.

He stared at the ground as he tried to wrap his mind around the twisted problems of his past and what Breanna was telling him now. He shook the thoughts away.

"I wouldn't fall," he joked.

"I wouldn't have either." She leveled her gaze at him. "That scoundrel pushed me. I thought I saw a knife— that's how he unbalanced me."

Anger coursed through him. "Did he say anything?"

She brushed off her pants and walked toward her horse, gingerly at first, but then her stance relaxed. She seemed unharmed, but how was that possible?

She shook her head, now settling the horse with one hand at its neck, bending to check each hoof.

"Ride down?" she asked.

"I think I'll hike." It would take him at least that long to regain his composure.

She accepted a hand up into the saddle and then began picking her way down the hillside. He did the same on foot.

Why would Scar-face have pushed Breanna? He'd winded his horse just to get close. She was one of the top competitors. That much was evident by her daily rides. Maybe the man had wanted her out of the race?

Whatever his reason, Adam wasn't going to let this stand.

The race master hadn't taken action when her stirrups had been cut, but Adam would see to it that the man did now. Or maybe even the nearest sheriff. As far as he was concerned, pushing her off her horse on a hill was attempted murder. And no one threatened his woman and got away with it.

He joined her at the bottom of the hill, and they walked their horses to the creek. He was still so furious, he couldn't think of a word to say.

By now he knew the routine. Pour water on the horses. Check their tack. Check their hooves. Good thing he could do all that without needing to pay much attention.

"Are you all right?" she asked.

He glanced at her.

She added, "You look a little..."

"Murderous?" he supplied when she didn't seem to want to name the emotion boiling just beneath his skin.

She laughed, but he wasn't joking.

"No one hurts my woman."

She remained near her horse, one hand on its shoulder. "Am I yours, then?"

He'd often heard a current of humor beneath her words, but not now. She studied him from beneath long lashes.

"You asked me to go back to Bear Creek with you," he reminded her. "As far as I'm concerned, that was an admission that we belong together. We just haven't decided on the *where*."

He thought he saw a soft smile before she turned her face away. She watched her horse lowered its head and drink.

"Do you really think we belong together?" Her voice seemed to soften somehow over the words. "I barely scraped by in a one-room schoolhouse, and you're..."

She gestured toward him.

But, no. He didn't know what she was referring to. "Unspeakably handsome?" he offered.

She crinkled her nose at him. "You're a writer, and... well read."

He shrugged. "You've got much more animal sense than I do. You could probably survive on the land for months if you had to. I don't have those skills."

She rolled her eyes. "I'm sure all the ladies at your fancy Philadelphia parties will want to hear about animal husbandry and crops."

"What parties? What women?" He'd admitted to his mother's matchmaking, but— "I rarely attend social events. I doubt I'll have time at all after I take over the paper. And anyway, do you honestly care what those imaginary women might think of you?" It seemed ludicrous that the Breanna he knew would be worried about such a thing.

She shrugged, avoiding eye contact.

Something deep in his gut told him to slow down. To follow this rabbit trail, however incongruent it felt.

He stepped closer to her. "You and I have plenty enough to talk about, don't we?"

"For now." She glanced at him, but it was brief.

"You think I'll get bored being with you?" He had to laugh. "Breanna, you are the least boring person I know."

Now the glance she turned on him was pointed. "I'm a novelty to you."

He took another step toward her, this time stopping when he was close enough to reach out for her. He did, snaking one arm around her waist.

She didn't resist but came into his arms.

"You aren't a novelty to me." The thought that he could ever find her boring made him want to chuckle, but he knew that in this intimate moment, she wouldn't appreciate his humor.

"You surprise me," he said. "Constantly. That you would risk your race to save the young Johnson boy." He brushed a few wayward strands of hair from her face. "That you could even feel threatened over what someone might think of you."

Some shadow passed through her expression.

"What is it?" he asked.

The... vulnerability, perhaps? Whatever it was, it fled in the face of his gentle query.

Her gaze changed. Sharpened, somehow, as her glance fell to his lips.

"Why haven't you claimed your boons?" she whispered.

Holding her close like this, a kiss seemed inevitable. All he had to do was drop his head and take it.

Kissing her again had been on his mind for days. It was all he wanted...

But it wasn't, not really.

He tried to keep his head, but it was a near thing. "I keep telling myself that if I let you come to me, the reward will be sweeter. I frightened you off once..."

He squeezed her and then let her go.

She was looking at him strangely as they gathered up their reins and prepared to go.

"What?"

She shook her head.

A look that curious couldn't go unnoticed. "Tell me." He hadn't meant to sound demanding. Or maybe he had.

"I can't decide whether I should be charmed or offended. You sounded like you were wooing an unbroken colt."

He couldn't help laughing, because once again, she'd managed to surprise him.

"Be charmed," he called out to her as he kicked his stallion into a canter.

He had a woman to protect, and he meant to do it right.

It was hot the next day and Breanna had insisted on extra breaks for the horses.

She was constantly on the lookout for Scar-face. His friend hadn't checked in the night before, and no one seemed to know where he was. Out of the fifteen competitors left, Scar-face had been there, bunking down in the church building.

Her head was pounding. Maybe from squinting into the harsh sunlight.

Neither Breanna or Adam had been able to locate the race master. Someone said he'd gone ahead to set up the finish line in Chicago, but no one was quite sure. He'd left an assistant to check in the racers, but the pimpled boy was barely eighteen and had been no help when she and Adam had tried to report what had happened out on that slope.

Adam had gone for the sheriff next, only to find the

man and his deputies out hunting a bank robber who'd been through a day earlier.

Adam had not been happy when he'd returned to the livery to report it.

They'd bedded down with their horses again, and she'd been so exhausted there had been no conversation before she'd nodded off.

I keep telling myself that if I let you come to me, the reward will be sweeter. Adam's words from yesterday had played in her mind over and over through the course of the morning.

She joked with him about being treated like a horse he wanted to break, but really, she was charmed. He was considerate, not trying to push his own feelings on her, though she knew he still hoped she'd decide to return home with him.

She'd begun to hope for herself that he would return to Bear Creek with her.

She'd felt off all morning. A little shaky. A strange buzz beneath her skin. If she didn't know better, she'd think a seizure was imminent. But she hadn't had one in almost four years. That letter from Millie—Breanna would never call the woman *mother*—had said the seizures should stop when Breanna reached her majority. Maxwell had confirmed it, citing numerous case studies of individuals with seizures only when they were children.

But the foreboding feeling remained.

By noon, the feeling worsened.

She had to get off the horse. And she had to get rid of Adam. He couldn't see her in the throes of a seizure.

She's got a demon inside her. She ain't all right in the head. Someone with a condition like hers shouldn't be in the classroom. Voices from her childhood clamored in her mind, and she only knew one thing. If Adam saw her having a seizure, whatever attraction he felt for her would disappear completely.

And though a few days ago, she thought that was what she wanted, now she couldn't bear it.

While occasionally the seizures surprised her, she sometimes had an intuition in the few moments before. Like now.

She prayed for deliverance, like she had so many times before. And knew that it wasn't coming.

She reined in near a copse of trees. It was the only shelter on this vast stretch of plain, and she hoped it would be enough to hide her from Adam.

He reined in behind her.

"Just... stay," she demanded. Drat. Her voice was shaking.

He looked curious.

She didn't have time for explanations, and she didn't want him to be curious.

She slipped off of the gelding's back and put the horse between herself and Adam, hoping he couldn't see the way her hands were shaking or see the lie on her face.

"I have... I need a few moments to myself. For womanly reasons," she blurted.

Of all the things she could've said! But that excuse would've curbed the curiosity out of her brothers.

"Do you—"

"No!" She pushed away from the horse as the tingling sensation at the back of her neck grew worse.

She didn't have long now. She needed...

She slipped through the trees, once stopping to brace herself against a sapling. She bent and picked up a thick twig from the ground. Kept walking. A few more paces.

She could feel the weakness taking over her limbs—

There.

Behind the copse of trees the plains spread out before her. A stone had been laid there by the hand of God maybe, but it was big enough that it should hide her completely, even if Adam came looking for her. The seizures usually only lasted a couple of minutes.

She lay in the grass, hating this. Hating herself. She put the twig between her teeth and bit down, knowing that it would be better to bite down on it rather than on her tongue or lip.

Her eyes remained open to the expanse of blue sky above as the seizure took over her body. Her limbs shook, her torso, even her head beat down against the grassy earth.

Don't let Adam seek her out.

Don't let him see.

. . .

SOMETHING WAS AMISS. Adam shifted in his saddle, unsure whether he should follow Breanna or leave her be.

Womanly reasons, she'd said. But her eyes had cut down and to the right, a sign she might be lying. He'd read the sign before when hunting down a story for his father.

What if she needed help? He'd been on edge all day, knowing Scar-face was still in the race, somewhere out there.

He'd seen the man ahead of them earlier, crossing the horizon, but it didn't mean he wouldn't double back. He seemed to have some sort of vendetta against Breanna. Personal or just trying to win, Adam didn't know.

He kicked his leg over the saddle and got his boots on the ground.

Go after her? Or stay and wait?

"Breanna?" he called out.

The copse of trees wasn't large. Not a forest by any means. He could see through it to the other side, blue sky and more grass.

But he couldn't see her.

"Breanna. Answer me, darling."

If he'd hoped to get a rise out of her, the endearment hadn't done it. She gave no response.

Where had she gone? She couldn't have just disappeared.

Unease tightened his gut. He didn't like this. What if she truly needed help?

"Breanna, if you don't answer, I'm coming after you."

Still nothing. He gave her another count of ten and then strode into the trees toward where she'd disappeared.

The copse provided little shade, not nearly enough to combat the day's heat. He turned on his heel, looking in all directions. She wasn't beneath the trees.

Then where had she gone?

He wandered out the other side, seeing only sky and grass and what seemed to be endless plain. No Breanna.

Except...

He took a step closer. Was that her boot, sticking out from behind a singular boulder rising from the ground?

It was. Why hadn't she answered him?

She must be lying down, if he couldn't see the top of her hat above the rock. Was she injured?

"Breanna—"

He couldn't stand it. It didn't matter that she'd asked him to wait. He rounded the rock, praying he wasn't about to intrude on a private moment. But if that were the case, then why hadn't she answered?

What he found stopped him cold. She was on the ground, her body convulsing.

"Breanna!" He dropped to his knees at her side. He didn't know whether to reach for her or not.

He caught sight of the stick between her teeth. Like

she'd known this attack was coming and had prepared as best she could.

The way her body was spasming, he was afraid to move her.

He took of his hat and shaded her face from the worst of the sun.

"It's all right. I'm here."

He smoothed back her hair from her forehead and saw the tracks left by her tears slipping down the sides of her face.

"It's all right," he repeated.

IT'S ALL RIGHT.

Breanna heard his words, but she wouldn't believe in them. How could she, when he'd seen her at her weakest?

She couldn't seem to stem the flow of tears that had started when he'd called out, *If you don't answer, I'm coming after you.*

She hated this sickness that caused her body not to be her own. Hated it.

The seizure slowly began to fade, and she was left with muscles worn weak from their ordeal. She closed her eyes. She couldn't bear to see whatever expression would be on Adam's face. She turned her head and let the stick fall from her lips.

Even her jaw ached as she closed her lips. She left her head turned. She couldn't bear to look at him.

She felt a tickle at her wrist, and then his hand clasped hers, his hold warm and tender.

More tears seeped from her closed eyes.

"Am I meant to be scared off now?" he asked quietly.

She felt him shift beside her, felt him looming above her.

"I suppose this is the secret you've been keeping that puts a shadow in your expression every time Philadelphia is mentioned."

He sounded so much the *same*. So calm and unruffled that her emotions overflowed.

"It isn't!" she burst out. She sat up suddenly, and he rocked back to keep their heads from bumping.

She tried to scramble to her feet, but her muscles gave way. She cursed the weakness as she settled onto the huge rock.

Adam remained where he was, kneeling in the grass, giving her the position of power. For once, his expression was totally inscrutable. She couldn't read him at all.

The man pushed and he *pushed*. She'd asked him to wait by the horses and he'd refused.

He'd stumbled on one of the two things that shamed her most. And now—

"You won't be content until you have all my secrets, will you?" She scrubbed her face with the sleeve of her shirt, stemming her tears by sheer force of will.

Adam simply waited, unspeaking, looking up at her from the grass.

"Take it, then," she said bitterly. "I was adopted by

my Pa when I was born. And a good thing, too, because it seems my birth family would've been content to throw me away, no matter who or what would take me."

He shook his head, uncomprehending.

So she began from the beginning. "My pa was a bricklayer's apprentice. He worked on a project next to a girls' finishing school, and though he'd never said one word to any of the students there, my birth mother claimed they'd..." She couldn't quite say the words and made a gesture she hoped would suffice. "When her parents confronted Pa, he lost his job and the credibility he'd begun to build for himself. My birth grandparents paid him off to take me away quietly. So that my *mother*"—she snarled the word—"could still have a society marriage. They had to have known that he wasn't my real father." She shook her head, tears pressing against the back of her throat. "He could've been anyone. A monster. A thief. And they gave me over to him anyway."

It had been the best thing that ever could've happened to her. Pa had grown up on the streets, abandoned by his own family. It had made him determined that every child had worth. He'd fought judgments from neighbors, the unyielding Wyoming weather, and his own self-worth to give the children he'd accepted as his own a good life.

"I confronted them in Philadelphia three years ago," she told Adam, who was still listening with rapt attention. "My birth grandparents. The man who'd thrown me away looked right into my face and said, 'I have no granddaughter.'"

The words still stung, though she'd done her best to stuff the memories and the accompanying pain away in a dark and tiny corner of her heart.

It was still enough to take her breath away.

She had no more words anyway. Now he knew everything.

"So Philadelphia has broken your heart," he said quietly.

She looked sharply at him. "I don't break." Though tears threatened, stinging the back of her nose.

"Philadelphia is a large city," he finally said, though his eyes were hooded. "I doubt you would ever see them—"

"My birth family could be your next-door neighbors. God knows they had enough money to erase my birth completely. They are just the kind of people who'd move in the same circles you do."

It didn't bear thinking about. This could never work.

And yet Adam remained on his knees, that stubborn tilt of his chin showing he wasn't willing to give an inch, even now that he understood.

"The kind of people who attend fancy parties," she said with a flutter of her hand in her lap. "The kind who would take one look at your new country wife and then act as if I didn't exist. Or worse, start whispers so that then everyone in your acquaintance knows—"

"I don't care!" He sprang up from the ground. "If you think for one moment that I care about the opinions of anyone who doesn't really know you"—he expelled a frustrated breath—"you'd be wrong. I could throttle your family for making a little girl and then a young woman feel abandoned." He ran both hands through his hair, his hat forgotten on the grass. "I care about you, Breanna. I can't help but admire the woman you've become. You've overcome so much and you haven't let yourself become bitter."

She stood as he spoke. He was being ridiculous. She'd told him everything, and he still didn't understand.

"I can't go back with you—"

He stepped right up to her. Maybe it was the fierce light in his eyes, or maybe she was still weak from her seizure, but she wobbled on her feet. His hands came to her waist.

"I'm falling in love…"

She couldn't let him say it.

She leaned against his chest, went up on tiptoe, and pressed her lips to his to stop the flow of words.

He met her with a fierce tenderness that stole her breath and made her weak all over again. But he held her close, his strong hands spanning her waist. His steady strength was exactly what she needed.

She clung to him. A woman who never wanted to depend on anyone else. She should have stepped away. She absolutely shouldn't have encouraged the emotions that had already built between them.

But the press of his lips, the sweep of his tongue, the touch of his nose against her cheek. All of it conspired to make her dizzy and wanting and falling...

He broke the kiss, but not his hold on her. If anything, he tucked her closer as they panted for breath. Her chin pressed into his shoulder, and she stared blindly at the landscape behind him.

"I can't," she whispered into the material of his vest. Whether he heard her, she didn't know.

I can't. Return to Philadelphia. Be his wife. Face those people.

Adam thought her someone brave, even courageous, but she wasn't.

She wasn't enough to be his wife, and now they both knew it.

12

The next morning dawned rainy and dreary. This wasn't the cool drizzle they'd endured during the early days of the race, but a downpour that made it difficult to see more than a few yards ahead.

Yesterday afternoon, Breanna had been quiet and pensive. Adam didn't know and hadn't asked whether her episode had exhausted her. He suspected it had. Not only physically, but emotionally as well.

She'd told him her last secret, and her refusal to travel home with him had made a sick kind of sense. No wonder she didn't want to return to Philadelphia after being so soundly rejected. Rejected by the ones who were supposed to love her the most.

Breanna had carried this all her life. He couldn't expect her to overcome it in the span of a few days or with a few reassuring words from him.

Could her fears and hurt be overcome?

She trusted and deeply loved her adoptive family.

Jonas and Penny had earned that trust and given Breanna a sense of security, but they'd had years of being there for her. Of proving themselves.

He had maybe thirty-six hours left with her before he needed to board an east-bound train.

If only he had more time.

He grimaced as his stallion splashed through a rolling creek. The cold water from below barely registered against his soaked pants.

As he walked beside her across yet another rolling plain, he considered the issue. Time was the one thing Breanna needed, and the one thing he didn't have. If he stayed on in Wyoming, it would buy him time to woo her properly, even celebrate a country wedding.

But at the cost of his father's health? If Father went back to work at the paper, the long hours and stress could kill him. Guilt would eat Adam alive, and then where would Reggie be? Abandoned and alone in Father's huge estate?

Adam loved Breanna.

But he also loved his father. He had a duty to his family.

There were no clear answers.

And though Breanna had kissed him good-night in the stable before they'd bedded down with their horses, it had felt like a goodbye.

He wasn't ready for good-bye. He'd only just found her, the independent, amazing, sometimes crazy-reckless woman who'd entirely captured his heart. How could he walk away?

Breanna drew up in front of him, and he reined in beside her, looking down the slight incline.

The rain had swollen what might've once been a creek or small tributary into a swiftly-flowing river overflowing its banks. The muddy current carried branches and other debris.

"Should we scout downstream?" he asked. "See if it widens to a better crossing?"

"No time," Breanna answered. "The rain's already cost us hours. It can't be that deep." She shot him a wry look. "It isn't as if we can get any wetter."

He looked at the swirling, muddy water. Back at her. "You sure?" It seemed like a big risk. But she was right. Time was short, and they'd been forced to slow because of the torrential rain.

She was sure, and he followed her down the muddy bank.

"You know how to swim, right?" she asked over her shoulder.

He nodded.

"If the water gets deep enough, slip off the side of your horse's saddle—don't let go— and just float along."

She made it sound easy, but this didn't look easy.

And then she was urging her horse forward, toward the water. He did the same, not wanting distance between them in case either of them needed help.

"It's not so deep," she called over her shoulder. A moment later, she called, "Never mind!"

He had only a brief moment to watch her glide off

of her gelding's back, floating as best she could fully clothed and with boots on.

He felt the moment the stallion's feet left solid ground. The horse sank beneath his weight, kicking all four legs.

He clung to the saddle with both hands but forced himself to kick with his legs and throw his body into the water. It was a chore to relax enough to float. He kicked, his boots heavy and water-logged.

They reached the other side without incident, Breanna sliding easily back into the saddle while he struggled for it, getting hit in the face with a rogue wave and taking on a mouthful of water.

Finally, the stallion finally dragged him into shallower water, where he could get a foothold.

He came up onto the bank coughing and spluttering, his hands on his knees. The stallion walked a few yards further from the water and stopped. Good thing, since Adam had lost the reins somewhere along the way.

Breanna hopped off her gelding as Adam flopped onto his back on the bank, finally drawing a clear breath.

"All good?" She stood behind his head and bent over him so that she appeared upside-down in his vision.

"I don't ever want to do that again."

She laughed. Her face was shining. Obviously the ordeal had energized her.

"I thought you said you'd encountered danger searching for your stories," she teased.

"I've never sought it out like that. We could've died."

"We didn't." She squatted down and smacked a kiss on his lips, nose bumping his chin, then was up again, bouncing on her toes.

She gave a wild war whoop, and the sound was enough to push him to climb to his feet.

He gave a wordless shout of his own and then went to her, grabbing her waist and twirling her in a dance no one on his acquaintance would recognize.

He didn't care.

She was shining up at him, her eyes alight and almost vibrating with joy. This time with her, *this moment,* was enough.

And then she was pulling away with a laugh. "Come on. We've got more riding to do."

A part of him couldn't wait for the race to be over. The misery of long hours in the saddle, chafing on days like today.

But another part, the bigger part, didn't want it to ever end.

Because when the race ended, so would his time with Breanna.

BREANNA HADN'T THOUGHT through the swim through that creek-river. She hadn't realized how close it would be for Adam.

She wasn't used to thinking about someone other than herself.

Perhaps another reason she shouldn't be thinking of

being with Adam. But then, Pa and Ma had made it work. They'd been from different worlds, Ma accustomed to luxury and Pa barely scraping by. Breanna had been five when they'd married, and she remembered several tense moments as they'd learned to navigate their new relationship.

There'd been shared laughter too, as they'd discovered in each other the perfect complement for themselves.

Breanna had been young and self-centered as most children could be. She'd never considered what it must've been like for her pa to have to trust Penny, an outsider, as she dealt with the makeshift family he'd already built.

Trusting Adam felt more frightening than jumping into that creek-river on her own without Buster's strength to guide her.

How had Pa done it? Her older brothers? Each of them had put hard work into their marriages—she'd seen it in action—and it showed. There was a mutual security and love beyond bounds.

She'd never thought she would find the same thing.

Could she trust Adam to guard her heart?

They were mounted up and walking their horses away from the creek when an indistinct shout from behind brought her head around.

There!

She reined in, aware of Adam beside her.

There was a horse in the water, caught and struggling beneath the visible branches of a huge root ball.

"A tree must've been swept into the water!" she said.

She urged her horse back to the bank. Adam followed.

She recognized the animal immediately, what with that white blaze across its face. It was Scar-face's horse.

But where was the man?

The horse broke free of the roots and swam for the opposite shore, soon finding its footing and getting out of the water.

Breanna pushed Buster close to the water's edge, straining her eyes as she looked for Scar-face in the swirling, roaring waters.

"Where is he?" she muttered to herself.

She didn't care for the man. He might be evil. He might've tried to kill her.

But that didn't mean he deserved to drown.

"There!" Adam called out. He was behind her and a little back from the water's edge. He pointed to the back side of the root ball, where a lump of black cloth —a body?—seemed to be caught.

She reached for the lariat tied to her saddle and freed it. It was the work of a moment to work up a good loop above her head.

How long had the man been under water? Was it already too late?

She would have maybe one shot at this before the rapid current would bear the man away. No guarantee that she could even find something to rope. She wouldn't be able to hold the tree itself. It was too big, too heavy.

And then somehow the tree rotated, just slightly. But enough that the tip of one booted foot jutted out of the water.

She sent the lasso flying. Her aim was true. The loop snagged around the floating boot, and she was quick to jerk the loop tight. She'd got him!

But the current was flowing with too much force. Even Buster couldn't brace against the weight of that massive tree being sucked away by the creek-river.

She was going to have to let go of her rope.

Unless—

"Don't even think it," Adam called out. "You aren't going back in the water. Not after that scum."

She opened her mouth to explain. If Adam held the rope, she could swim near Scar-face and knock him free off the tree roots.

It was risky. Possibly she could get sucked into the same trap, caught in the tree. But if they didn't do anything, the man would die!

"There," Adam shouted.

She glanced at him to see him pointing at a spit of land that jutted out into the creek. It was coming up fast.

"If we both brace from there, maybe we can break him free."

It was as good an idea as any, only this way they'd stay out of the dangerous waters.

She galloped her gelding and met him on the spit of land. She looped the rope around her gloved hands and tossed Adam the end. She wouldn't risk her horse by tying it around the saddle.

"Here it comes!" she called out.

And the tree was upon them.

"Let some slack build in," Adam said. Good idea.

The rope went slack as the tree neared and then passed.

"Now!"

And she and Adam gave a mighty heave at the same moment the rope went taut.

And miraculously, Scar-face broke free of the debris.

Breanna pulled on the rope hand-over-hand as Adam hopped off his horse and moved to the water's edge.

Her arms were burning with the strain, and Adam seemed to know, looking back to her and nodding as he grabbed the rope from where he stood and gave a good heave. Another pull. And another, and then Scar-face was close enough for Adam to wade into the water and lift him onto the shore.

Adam flopped the man onto his back, and Breanna curbed any protest she might've made. It wasn't as if he deserved kind treatment after what he'd done to her.

Scar-face's skin was gray, and his mouth was slack. He wasn't conscious.

"Is he alive?" Adam asked, breathing hard.

She bent over the man. Maxwell would know how to take his pulse, but all she knew to do was put her ear to his chest. All she heard was the sound of the rain beating down on them. No breathing.

"Can you help me turn him on his side?"

Adam was beside her before she'd finished the question, rolling the man onto his side. Breanna gave him a good whack between the shoulder blades. Another. Three. Five. Ten.

Adam let go, the man slumping back to the ground, limp.

"I don't think—"

But she didn't have a chance to hear what Adam thought because Scar-face lurched and began retching up copious amounts of disgusting muddy water.

Adam tipped him over to his belly with his toe as the man flailed, fighting for breath.

Smart.

Scar-face had proved himself wily and dangerous.

Breanna backed up a step, prepared to jump into the saddle if the man moved a finger in her direction.

He didn't. He looked weak as a baby as he struggled to a sitting position right there on the bank.

Adam exchanged a glance with her. "I think we're done here."

She agreed. They'd saved the man, and that was enough.

"Where's... horse?" Scar-face asked breathlessly.

Adam pointed to the opposite bank, where the horse with the white blaze waited with empty saddle.

Breanna swung up onto her gelding's back. Adam did the same with his stallion.

It might be hours until the creek subsided. Or days.

It appeared the race had one fewer rider.

And Scar-face seemed to know it. They were already yards away when Breanna caught his cold, calculating glance.

"Terrible manners," Adam said as they began to walk their horses, leaving the man sitting where he was. "Not even a thank-you for saving his life."

"We don't need his thanks," she returned. "That wasn't why we did it."

He winked at her. He knew. "If it were up to me, I'd have let him drown."

"You wouldn't have."

He shrugged, and his expression was inscrutable again. She'd never forget the look he'd worn after Scar-face had knocked her from her horse.

Maybe he would've let Scar-face drown.

But at least neither of them would have a stain on their conscience.

She'd been clutching the rope in one hand, eager to put some distance between herself and the creek, and now she began looping it.

"That was some fine roping," he said with a nod to her rope. "The best I've seen."

She felt a slow flush rise into her cheeks. Felt suffused with pleasure at his praise. "Exactly how much roping have you witnessed?"

He winked. "Enough."

She had half a mind to send a loop over his shoulders but thought that might just encourage him.

"You were cool under pressure," she said. "Good idea about using that spit of land."

Not everyone could keep his head in a life-or-death situation.

"I told you I wouldn't go swimming in that creek again."

She rolled her eyes, grateful for the man beside her.

They picked up the horses' pace, and as they raced through the muddy terrain toward the last check-in, she imagined herself having many more adventures with the man beside her.

The question was, between the rain that had slowed them and they time they'd spent saving Scar-face, would they be able to beat the sunset check-in? It was hard to tell as the hours passed with the rain pouring down on them. It would be a near thing.

Even if they made it to the check-in today, would she have anything left for the big push tomorrow? Twenty-four hours of riding would be nearly impossible under normal circumstances, and these were anything but.

She glanced over at Adam, whose eyes were squinted against the rain.

They'd almost made it. Another thirty-six hours, and he'd be leaving for home.

Though she'd bared her heart to him, neither one had made any promises.

He hadn't asked her to go back with him in days.

She wouldn't say yes if he did.

Would she?

. . .

SEB,

I AM TERRIBLY SORRY. When I departed Bear Creek, I left you with the impression that there could be something between us. I am not in love with you and I never will be. I am quite content with my life here and never intend to return to Bear Creek. Please don't write me again. There is nothing left to say.

Emma

SEB CRUMPLED THE LETTER. He balled it in his fist and let it fly across the bunkhouse. Didn't matter that he'd missed the stove. He was the only one left to sleep in here, with his brothers all married off.

And now Breanna had a beau. Maybe she'd even go off to Philadelphia. Seb was the only one alone.

And Emma had no intention of that changing.

Pain stabbed through his head, and his eyes were hot. With a jolt, he realized he was... crying? He swiped at his cheeks with the back of his wrist.

I am not in love with you and I never will be.

How could he have been so wrong? He'd seen the emotions in her eyes when she looked up at him. He'd felt it in her touch. She had cared about him. He'd have bet his life on it.

Had something happened since she'd left? Maybe

she'd met someone. Someone smart, like Daniel.

Someone better suited to her.

His breath sawed in and out of his chest. He'd already started building the foundation for a little cabin in his and Emma's grove. No way could he finish it now. He could never live there—alone or with someone else.

He wasn't even sure he could stay on the homestead, with memories of Emma at every turn. They'd only had a short time together, but she'd been a part of the family for three years. Gone berry picking with Breanna and come back with stained fingers and skirt. Learned to fish. Swam and splashed in the creek after harvest with the rest of them.

She was everywhere.

So maybe he couldn't be here anymore.

13

It was still dark outside the livery as Breanna readied her horse for the last leg of the race.

This was it.

Her chance to win five hundred dollars. How many adventures could she go on with that much capital? Or maybe she'd purchase the horse of her dreams.

Or buy a train ticket to Philadelphia.

The other riders, eleven left, were quiet as they too readied their horses. Adam was in the stall next to hers.

And then he appeared in the doorway, knocked once softly on the frame. His hat was off, his hair mussed. His eyes were tired.

He looked as rough as she felt. She couldn't wait to sleep in a real bed again.

Adam stepped close.

Breanna glanced around, but none of the other cowboys were paying them any attention.

"I thought I'd better collect my good luck kiss now," he said.

She stepped into his arms and rested her hands against his shoulders.

He bent his head close to hers, nuzzling her ear with his nose. The whiskers at his jaw caught in the fine hairs at her temple.

"I thought you were saving your boons to collect later," she whispered as a delicious shiver ran down her spine.

He pressed his face into her neck. "Later is coming too soon," he murmured.

Wasn't that the truth?

And then he moved back slightly and looked into her face. He smiled slightly. "For luck."

And he kissed her.

Everything fell away. There were no other riders. No day- and night-long ride waiting for her. No difficult decisions.

Only Adam.

Only his hands firm on her waist. Only the press of his mouth against hers. Only his scent in her nose and his strength beneath her hands.

She wanted more than this moment. More than today.

She wanted forever.

It was she who broke away this time, pressing her face into his shoulder to hide the sudden tears that filled her eyes.

Somehow he knew, because one of his hands moved

to cup the nape of her neck, his fingers sliding into the braid there.

"It'll work out," he whispered against her temple.

He gave her a moment to compose herself and then set her away, though he kept his hands at her waist.

"I want a new wager," he said.

She wiped her cheeks with both hands, afraid he'd see a remnant of her tears. Then she placed her hands on his forearms. "What kind of wager?"

"You've carried me this far in the race. I think you should race this last leg on your own, no city boy holding you back."

She narrowed her eyes. "You mean you're going to try to beat me?"

There was a definite ornery sparkle in his eyes—one she'd come to recognize from her brothers—as he smiled down at her. "I suppose you could say that."

She felt a grin coming on. One she couldn't suppress in the face of his own contagious smile.

"And if you win?" There was no way she was going to let that happen, but let him think it was in the realm of possibility.

"If I win," the merriment faded from his face. "You'll come to Philadelphia with me. On a trial basis," he added quickly when she opened her mouth to protest.

Or had she been going to agree?

"If you hate it, or if you tire of me, then I'll pay for a train ticket to send you home."

She started to shake her head, not even sure what

she was disagreeing with. Maybe that crazy notion that she could ever tire of him.

But the riders around them began moving in earnest toward the door.

Out on the street, there would be a small crowd waiting to send them off.

She arched up on the toes of her boots and kissed him one more time.

"You'll never beat me," she whispered and felt his smile against her lips.

"So that's a yes?"

She winked at him just before he backed out of the stall and left her to mount up.

Buster was antsy, probably feeling the tension she carried in her entire body.

They exploded from the starting line when the pistol cracked.

The cowboys broke into a gallop as one, everyone neck and neck until they cleared the last building in town and spread out.

She broke away from the pack, Adam tailing her.

And then he winked and doffed his hat before spurring his stallion into a canter. He quickly outpaced her, but that was okay. She'd planned her race and wouldn't allow him to derail her now.

He was disappearing over the horizon when she realized he'd never mentioned what she would win if she beat him to Chicago.

What was her prize when she won?

He'd told her in plain terms that he couldn't stay in Wyoming, not with his father so ill.

It'll work out, he'd said.

How could it, when they both had separate ways to go?

He'd trusted her to lead yesterday when they'd saved Scar-face. Been at her side and instrumental in getting the man to shore.

Could she trust him to lead in this? In whatever next step would come for their relationship?

BREANNA WAS two miles into the last leg of the race when Buster came up lame. His limp was pronounced. She didn't want to push him for more than a walk back to town, for fear he'd be injured worse.

She was somewhere in the middle of the pack of riders. She'd trusted that her gelding would make up time as each horse's endurance was put to the test.

But her ride was at an end. She would never kill her horse trying to win.

Archie Johnson rode past her, raising his hand in a half wave. He didn't even slow.

Adam might win. She hadn't seen him since this morning, when he'd ridden away first thing. He was somewhere ahead. He wouldn't even know she'd lost until he reached the finish line.

She led Buster by his reins in a slow walk back toward town. A few hours and they would reach it. She could take the train to Chicago, maybe meet up with Adam there.

And then...

Go with him to Philadelphia?

Maybe it was better this way. The wager had seemed ridiculous at the time, because she'd been so certain of winning.

But if Adam won, the decision would be out of her hands.

He'd promised he wouldn't pressure her to stay. Had her previous visit been colored entirely by her grandfather's rejection?

What if she could find happiness there?

What if everything happened the way she'd imagined since she'd met Adam? Fancy ladies rejecting her outright, Adam becoming ashamed of her.

It could be awful.

Or it could be wonderful. Like dancing in the rain. Like kisses at sunrise.

She took off her hat and slapped it against her thigh. This uncertainty was enough to make her crazy.

And then the sound of galloping hoofbeats brought her head around.

"Halloo!"

She whirled to find Adam on the approach, riding toward her, riding in the wrong direction. At least if he wanted to win the race.

"What's the matter?" He reined in and dismounted almost in one movement, expression worried.

"He's lame in his front foreleg. Our race is over."

Adam strode up to her and wrapped his arms around her. She clung to him for only a moment. She could allow herself that long to lament the race she wouldn't win.

She pushed away from him. "You'd better get going. Buster and I'll take the train to Chicago, maybe even watch you cross the finish line." She tilted her head to the side. "How'd you know to come back, anyway?"

" I was taking a short break for water when Johnson told me you were walking. Are you sure he can't continue?"

She nodded even as Adam went back to his horse. Probably ready to saddle up.

But he began unlashing his saddlebags.

"What are you doing?"

He kept at it. "You're riding Domino. I offered him to you before the race started. He'll help you win. He's got it in him."

Hot moisture pooled in her eyes, and she quickly blinked it away. "I can't—"

"Of course you can." Now he moved to her gelding and began to unlash her saddlebags. "The rules were that you could have two horses as part of the race." He shrugged. "I just rode your second until this point."

ADAM HAD KNOWN what he had to do from the moment the older Johnson brother had told him Breanna was walking her horse back toward town.

Now she was looking at him as if he were crazy as

he held out her saddlebags to her, waiting for her to secure them and then ride off on Domino. Maybe he was crazy. He kept remembering her fall from the horse. What if she fell again? Scar-face and his friend were out of the race, so it wasn't a worry that one of them would try to attack Breanna again. Anything could happen.

But he couldn't hold her back.

She didn't reach for the saddlebags. "Adam, I can't."

She'd told him her most secret dreams. Traveling and adventure and *family*. All right, that one he'd figured out on his own.

Maybe he couldn't give her adventure, at least not more than this race, but he could give her this. The prize money would be a start for her.

She needed to win. For herself.

So he took the step between them. He pressed the leather satchels into her hands. "You started this. Finish it." He kissed her temple and gently untangled the gelding's reins from her fingers.

"I'll watch over him for you. We'll see you in Chicago."

He started walking backwards. She still hadn't moved, was looking at him with luminous eyes.

"He'll try to pull the reins out of your hands. Don't let him pull rank on you."

Her lips lifted in a small smile.

She shook her head, then stepped toward Domino. It was quick work for her to tie off her saddle bags and adjust the stirrups.

Adam kept walking backward so he could have one last look at his cowgirl as the fierce determination she'd begun the race with returned to her features..

"Godspeed," he called out.

She lifted one hand. Wheeled the horse, though she didn't gallop away like he'd expected.

"Adam!"

He doffed his hat to her.

"Thank you!"

Her voice carried on the wind, and then she was gone. They were beauty in motion, like he'd known they would be. They were a match in temperament and will.

She was going to win.

She hadn't brought up his silly wager. It had been a long shot for him anyway. He'd gotten this far in the race only because of Breanna.

It'll work out, he'd told her in the livery. She'd been soft and warm in his arms, and he'd dared to hope.

But he didn't know how to make it work.

He only knew that she had to win, and he'd made it happen for her. It would have to be enough.

THE STALLION LOPED AWAY, his stride eating up the grassy plain, leaving Adam behind with Buster.

She couldn't explain the tears leaking from the corners of her eyes.

Maybe it was the sheer majesty of his horse. Each stride was smooth, each beat of hooves against the ground like war drums, thrumming through her entire body.

Domino was meant to race. Even with what they'd endured so far, he had a reserve of strength that hadn't been tapped.

Maybe she couldn't have beaten Adam after all, not with this magnificent horse.

But it wasn't the communion of woman and animal that was making her emotional.

It was Adam, sacrificing his chance to win for her.

None of her brothers would've done it. Not even Matty. They'd have waved goodbye and not looked back.

She didn't understand Adam, hadn't from the beginning.

But she was learning that perhaps that wasn't a bad thing. Learning Adam was an adventure in itself.

Was it one that she could enjoy for the rest of her life?

14

Breanna did lash herself to the saddle in those darkest hours of the night. The Lord had coordinated a half moon to light their way, but after six days of hard riding and now riding overnight, Breanna had no strength to keep her eyes open.

She dozed, sometimes coming to in order to make sure Domino was still on the right heading.

The stallion was incredible. Tired, of course, as they walked part of the way.

But he was giving her everything he had.

She had passed by two of the other riders. Knew at least three others were behind her.

How many were ahead? Or was she in first place?

She dozed again, momentarily forgetting her worries about winning.

She dreamed. Of being in Adam's arms in some fancy ballroom, of enough eyes on them to make her uncomfortable. And then pointing fingers from faceless bodies, laughs and jeers. And then Adam let her go, stepped back and joined the crowd, a sneer on his handsome face.

She awoke with a start as the stallion splashed into a shallow creek.

How long had it been since they'd taken a break?

She reined in and let him take a good, long drink. She untied the bindings at her thighs that were keeping her in the saddle, slid down from the horse, her boots splashing in the shallow water.

She knelt and cupped her hands in the icy water, splashed it on her face.

Was the dream only an expression of her own worries? Or a foretelling of what would come if she went to Philadelphia with Adam?

Back in the saddle, she lashed herself in again. There were hours still to go, and without anyone but the horse to talk to, it was best to secure herself.

She started singing, a trick Pa had taught her on a long-ago roundup. Her voice rang out loud and clear in the empty landscape. The stars wouldn't care that she couldn't carry a tune. The stallion didn't seem to, either.

She let him canter until her eyes were crossing with sleepiness again.

She wasn't aware she'd dozed, but this time the dream was different.

She was walking through an enormous house. Not one she recognized, but it was clear the furnishings were expensive and fine. A library—what would she do with that?—then a luxurious bedroom. And then a... nursery. Adam looked up at her from where he sprawled on the floor, his legs spread on a carpet. A toddler in a pinafore looked up and squealed with delight.

"Mama!" the little girl cried.

And Breanna startled awake again. Her breaths sounded harsh in the stillness.

The first rays of sunlight were gilding the horizon.

Sunrise—on the heels of that second dream. Could it be some kind of sign from above?

She'd never even thought past the humiliation waiting for her in Philadelphia to the life she and Adam could share. He'd never mentioned whether he wanted children, but she'd always wanted a big family. Maybe not as big and crazy as hers, but one or two children. Or three or four. Five, at the most.

Would Adam wear that soft look on his face, or had her imagination outdone itself?

Would he be the kind of father who spent all hours at the office, or the kind who spent all hours in the nursery?

He'd given her his horse. Sacrificed his race for hers.

Couldn't he see he was meant for more than wasting away in an office?

She caught sight of movement against the lightening horizon. A rider there. Either he'd passed her in the night or he'd been ahead of her all along.

They couldn't be far from the finish now. Maybe a

few miles. The other rider was at least a half a mile out and riding hard.

She touched the stallion's shoulder. "Are you awake, boy? We've got one more push."

He responded when she nudged him into a trot and then a full-out gallop.

Did he have enough energy left to catch that lone rider? To win?

Adam had caught a late train. It was the only one heading toward Chicago with an open stock car. He'd known that Breanna would never forgive him if he left Buster behind, so he'd done his best to sleep on the overnight train in a crowded passenger car.

In the early morning hours, he couldn't help straining his eyes to see out into the darkness. She was out there somewhere. Was she taking care of herself? Stopping enough?

The train ride both took forever and wasn't long enough. He still hadn't discovered a solution to the worlds that seemed to be pulling them in opposite directions.

He disembarked at the Chicago station, trying to shake off his exhaustion and keep his wits about him.

Get Buster. Send a quick telegraph to Clarence. Find his way to the finish line, which was set up on the outskirts of the sprawling city.

He'd have to hustle to make it there before the race ended. Already the sun was coming up.

Was Breanna in the lead? He prayed it was so. She'd wanted it so badly.

It took him longer than he'd thought to unload the gelding from the stock car ,and the station attendant was next to no help in giving directions to the race finish line. The boy was about Breanna's age and clueless that the event was even happening.

The sun was over the horizon by the time Adam settled Breanna's horse in an area well back from all the spectators. Someone—the race master?—had constructed a grandstand and the bleachers were filled, with more of a crowd spilling out at the ground level. Two flags had been placed twenty yards apart and fluttered in the early-morning breeze. Someone had painted a line between them, and a photographer stood waiting.

Would the race be so close they'd need the photo to know who won?

Adam joined the crowd spilling from the stands. He had a small notepad and that darn pencil stub in his hand, ready to send the final results back home as soon as possible.

He wouldn't get a good view of the riders as they approached, not until they got close. But he couldn't see a way to get up to the top.

A murmur rippled through the crowd, and he glanced up to the highest spectators to see several people pointing off in the distance.

He squinted against the morning sunlight, but couldn't make out a rider yet.

He glanced up into the stands. And then he had to do a double-take, because that was... was that Breanna's brother?

It was Seb.

He was sitting on the top of the bleachers, holding his little sister Ida on his shoulders.

Adam hoped someone was supervising the young man.

As he looked, he made out several other members of Breanna's family. Her father. Oscar and Sarah. Matty and Catherine. The baby was bundled on his papa's shoulder.

They'd come for her.

Of course they had. They were a closely knit family, and they supported her in ways he'd always wished he'd have received from his own father.

It meant that Adam's presence might be superfluous here.

If her family was here to welcome them back to their bosom, she didn't need him. They might talk her out of accompanying home.

He'd only ever had a small chance of getting her to agree since he'd withdrawn from the race, but he'd held onto that one kernel of hope.

Was her family's presence a good or a bad thing?

Before he had a chance to make up his mind, someone shouted his name from behind him. He turned to look, expecting another one of Breanna's brothers to have seen him.

But it wasn't one of the Whites at all.

. . .

BREANNA FLEW across the grassy plain, still several paces behind the cowboy she'd spotted as the sun rose. Johnson.

She'd gained on him incrementally as day had broken around them, had seen the moment he'd looked back and realized that someone was on his tail. He'd kicked his horse for more speed.

She'd done the same, amazed that Domino had anything left to give. He'd responded to her urging for more speed by lengthening his stride and pushing himself faster.

Would it be enough?

They gained on the cowboy inch by inch. The sun was coming up, glaring directly into Breanna's eyes. She tilted her head down so her hat brim blocked most of it.

On the horizon, buildings came into focus. Chicago.

Her heart pounded as a last surge of adrenaline pulsed through her. The stallion seemed to recognize it, or maybe he just wanted to be done with this endless ride. He seemed to stretch even lower to the ground, almost to fly.

Closer. Closer.

Still a stride behind the gray horse.

Over the rider's head she saw the flutter of a flag. Two flags. And a grandstand. Really?

And then it was only her heartbeat in her ears as the stallion gained another inch. Another.

They were neck and flank with the gray horse.

The finish line was right *there*.

She needed—

Domino leapt forward with one last burst of speed. She caught sight of Johnson's surprised expression— one that mirrored what she felt—as the flags flew past in her peripheral vision.

Had it been enough?

She was flying so fast that it took several dozen yards to rein in the stallion. She wheeled him in a long circle, the other rider following.

She finally reined in to a walk as they approached the finish line for a second time. It was teeming with people, and she dismounted as the race organizer ran out to meet them.

She ignored him for the moment and turned to shake Johnson's hand. "Good ride," she said.

"That's one incredible horse," he said, pumping her hand.

She had to wonder if she looked as beat-up as he did, face smudged with dirt and lined from exhaustion. She didn't want to breathe in too deeply, fearing what scent she'd pick up.

And then the race master was there, shaking first Johnson's hand and then hers.

"A fine finish!" the man crowed. "Couldn't have asked for a better one. Can't believe you pulled it out, little lady."

She hadn't been sure, not until this very moment. "I won?"

"You did," Johnson said with a tip of his hat. "Well done."

She felt the blood rushing in her ears and went a little lightheaded.

She'd won.

She'd really won.

"We'd like a photo with the two of you and your horses." The race master shooed back a whole gaggle of folks who'd approached behind him.

Breanna submitted to the photograph with what little patience she could muster. Where was Adam?

And then they were finished in a puff of smoke ,and the crowd teemed forward.

"My horse needs care" she said.

And then her brother Matty was there, sweeping her into a congratulatory hug. "I'll take care of 'im." Matty! What was her brother doing here?

He took the reins from her hands before she could protest. She was speechless.

And then she was surrounded by more of her family. Ma and Pa and Seb and Walt and... She lost count, laughing and crying as she was swarmed and hugged and passed from one to another.

"What happened to Buster?" Pa asked.

"Lame, just as we started this last leg," she said with a tearful gulp. She hated that she'd had to do it without her trusted horse. But—

"Adam took him. They were going to walk back to the nearest town. Have you seen him?"

She glanced around, but the crowd surged around them.

Pa shook his head.

"You're famous, sis!" Seb crowed, but there was an undertone in his voice she couldn't decipher. What was wrong with him?

He was smiling, but something was wrong. Something he was hiding.

Not that she had time to ask him about it, because a man in a tall hat was suddenly in her face. "I'm from the *Chicago Tribune*. I'd like to get a comment from the winning cowboy—er, cowgirl."

Here was a journalist, but not the one she wanted to see. Where was Adam?

Had he not made it in time?

15

It was at least a half hour before Breanna was able to break away from the press of the crowd and from her family.

She was drooping with exhaustion. All she wanted was the bed at the hotel.

And Adam.

Where was he?

Maybe he'd seen her family—and the crowd—and decided to bide his time. It wasn't exactly the place or time to convince her to hop on the train to Philadelphia.

The train.

Surely he hadn't gone already... No. He wouldn't go without Domino.

She'd check the livery first. The race master had rented several stalls for the riders' horses. Adam might be there. She couldn't imagine him leaving without

Domino, and really the animal needed rest as much as Breanna did. She would begin there.

The city was coming alive for the morning as Breanna followed the directions Matty had given her for the livery. Down the street and turn left.

A shopkeeper was out sweeping the sidewalk in front of his dry goods store. A woman in an apron washed the front windows of a millinery. The energy of the very city itself seemed to be waking up.

It energized Breanna.

It reminded her of the morning three years ago when she and Cecilia had walked along the streets in Philadelphia.

The very morning she'd met Adam.

Her thoughts were muddled. Why hadn't he come to her at the race's finish? Maybe he hadn't made the train.

She slipped inside the huge double doors of the livery and paused so her eyes, accustomed to the bright morning sunlight, could have a moment to adjust.

When they did, the sight brought relief that filled her like the wind catching her bonnet.

Adam was there.

The relief was promptly replaced by dismay when she saw who he was chatting with just outside Domino's stall.

It was a man in a wheeled chair so similar to the one Hattie used on occasion. And a woman in a dress that cost more than Breanna's prized saddle.

They hadn't seen her yet, and Breanna ducked

behind a partition. Her heart pounded in her ears, though she was so tired, the adrenaline rush at seeing Adam with... his family?...was minor compared to what she'd experienced in that final few minutes of the race.

Reggie had come to Chicago, though Adam had said he never left the house. Why?

Had something happened to Adam's father? Had they come to fetch him home?

If they had, why hadn't they already gone? Hopped a train and been on their way?

Breanna lifted her gaze above the partition and examined the woman standing between the men. Adam had said there was no one special for him back home. But then why was that woman touching him? Her hand rested lightly on Adam's forearm, and he didn't pull away.

She was smiling, though Breanna could only see her face in profile.

She was lovely. Her hair was dark and lustrous and pinned into a complicated style that Breanna could never hope to replicate.

And that dress! She didn't even know what fabric it was made of. Both smooth and shiny, it was pink and poufy and had extra bustles and black lace along the cinched waist. It probably cost more than everything Breanna owned added up together.

She didn't have to look down at herself to know what she looked like.

She wore dusty, dirty men's trousers. Her blouse and vest weren't in any better condition. Her hair was coming out of its braid, and she was in desperate need of a bath.

She looked like a country bumpkin, like the tomboy that she was.

She would never stand up next to someone like the woman in the pink dress.

Had she really even been contemplating it? Maybe Adam wasn't crazy. Maybe Breanna was the crazy one for thinking she could be what he needed.

What would his family, that woman, think if Breanna presented herself for introductions? They'd think she was ridiculous.

With the dream she'd experienced only hours ago, she couldn't bear to find out.

She ducked out of the livery, praying Adam wouldn't see her and come after her.

She had to escape.

"THERE. You've seen my magnificent stallion. Now tell me what this is all about."

Adam was standing next to the man, and he still couldn't believe Reggie had traveled all the way from Philadelphia.

He'd hugged his brother when he'd seen him on the street, so shocked that he'd barely been able to speak. At the finish line, they'd attempted to reach Breanna. But she'd been surrounded by onlookers and Reggie's chair had nearly been knocked over and Adam had been so puzzled by his brother's presence that he'd retreated to the stable. He'd given Matty a brief hello when the man had brought his horse and then quickly disappeared.

Reggie had first assured him that Father was fine. Then he'd claimed to have seen Adam's picture from at the starting line in a Chicago paper. Apparently, the story of the cowboy race had made it to their competitors first.

And for some reason, Reggie had convinced her nurse, Miss P., to attend him on the journey.

Though the look she exchanged with Reggie was anything but professional. "Shall I do some window shopping while you catch up with your brother?"

Reggie clasped her hand in his. "Stay."

Adam hadn't seen his brother wearing a look of such determination in years—not since before the accident.

Now Reggie's chin jutted up, and he met Adam's gaze squarely. "Miranda took me to task after Father fell ill."

Miranda? Ah. Miss P.

The two shared a glance.

"She'd been trying for months, I suppose." He took a breath. "I was lost in self-pity for far too long. Too focused on what I'd lost."

Miss P. squeezed his hand affectionately, and Reggie looked up at her. In his expression, there was an echo of the pain he'd shown for so long.

Adam's gut dropped like a stone. He'd caused this pain in Reggie.

"I'm sorry," he choked out.

Reggie shook his head. "There is nothing for you to be sorry for. I've been a pitiful mess all these years thinking I was broken." He smiled ruefully. "Miranda told me on her first day of employment that I should stop feeling sorry for myself. That I wasn't, in fact, dead and buried."

Adam knew his eyes widened even as Miss P. went pink. It was a bold thing to say to someone who could have you fired in an instant. Perhaps the nurse had more of a spine than her appearance would indicate.

Reggie gazed up at the woman, his emotion written clearly on his face. "It's taken some doing, but I've finally convinced her to marry me."

Adam was shocked all over again. He'd never imagined Reggie would come to him with news like this. He moved close to clasp his brother's hand and pump it. "Congratulations!"

The couple was all smiles as Adam stepped back.

Reggie, getting married. What did Mother think of it? Not that it mattered, not with Reggie shining with joy the way he was.

And then Reggie went serious, met Adam's gaze again. "I want to be the one to run the *Explorer.*"

It seemed it would be a morning for shock. This time, Adam felt the earth moving beneath him. "What?"

Reggie frowned. "You know I used to go with Father to the paper every day that Mother let me get away with it. I'd sit in the corner of his office and watch him work and dream of being there, behind the desk."

Reggie sighed. "For a long time, I thought it was beyond me. With my... limitations. But I've recently become convinced that I can do much more than I thought."

Adam glanced at Miss P., who was watching his brother with undisguised love. He recognized it because it mirrored what he felt for Breanna.

He was exceedingly proud of his brother. Reggie quite simply appeared to be a changed man. Just the journey to Chicago proved that. But—

"Father wants me to run the paper," Adam said quietly, not wanting to ruin his brother's newfound happiness but needing to speak the truth. Their father had been lying in his sickbed when he'd made the request.

Reggie leveled a look on him. "You can't tell me you want to sit in the old man's office day after day. Year after year."

Just the thought of it made Adam's stomach curdle.

"I promised Father I'd continue the family legacy," he said. He'd meant it. It owed it to Reggie. To Father. To Mother.

Reggie shook his head. "I told you," he muttered to Miss P.

The woman appeared just as serene as she had all morning. She met Adam's gaze squarely. "The newspaper is just a business, you know. The real legacy of the Cartwright family is you. And Reggie."

What a statement from someone he'd only met in passing, someone he'd barely acknowledged before today.

Where had she come from, this bold nurse?

"I've read every paper Father has put out in the last thirteen years," Reggie said. "And almost every copy of our competitors'. If you would be willing to help smooth things over in the office for a few months, I'm sure I could learn the management aspects—the machinery, handling the reporters. Just because I am in a chair doesn't mean I'm helpless."

For years, Adam would've argued with him. But there was a spark of life in Reggie that he recognized from the child his brother had been.

And a matching spark, deep in his breast. What if he *didn't* have to work in the stuffy office every day?

Just the thought of it was freeing.

"Father will never agree." It was a last, weak argument, and Reggie knew it.

His eyes were shining. "Father doesn't have to know, not at first. He's still bed-bound. I can prove myself for a few weeks, and then we can present the idea to him together. As a united front."

Adam crossed his arms over his chest. "And what am I to do instead of running the paper? Retire to the country?"

Reggie's eyes were dancing. "You could write. Articles or a novel or whatever. And you'd have time for proper courting."

Breanna. Where was she? He'd expected her before

now, but he'd been distracted by everything his brother had said.

Adam spun in a circle, pressing both hands to his temples. It was too much to take in. His exhausted brain couldn't fathom it.

"He's overwhelmed," said Miss P. with a little laugh, a sign of joy that he could easily see his brother being attracted to. "Maybe we should go to breakfast and talk some more."

"I need to find Breanna." Had she been waylaid by her family?

Had she decided to reject his suit entirely? Had she already been welcomed into their bosom? He'd expected her to seek him out. Was this silence her answer?

"Name the restaurant, and I'll catch up with you," he told them. "I have to find her."

BREANNA STRODE DOWN THE SIDEWALK, which was bustling now with people. She had no destination in mind, but she was receiving curious looks from nearly everyone she passed. No doubt it was the way she was dressed. Had anyone in Chicago ever seen a real cowgirl before?

Walking aimlessly wasn't going to fix anything.

But where should she go? Her parents had told her the name of the hotel where they'd rented rooms. She could go there and rest awhile. Even lie with a cold compress on her eyes like some dime-novel heroine.

She wished she could phone Cecilia, but she knew she'd have no privacy once she was back with her family. The children would be swarming around. Her brothers would want a full accounting of the danger she'd faced. And Pa would likely want reassurances that Adam hadn't compromised her in any way.

Cecilia would know what to do. She'd known almost from the moment she'd arrived in tow with Oscar and Sarah that she'd wanted to be a teacher. She'd gone after it with single-minded fervor.

Breanna didn't know what she wanted. Was it adventure that she longed for? Or Adam?

She was confused. And heartsick.

And then across the street, a woman on the sidewalk hailed her with a raised hand.

Ma.

"There you are." Ma was huffing as she bustled up to Breanna. "Going like the devil's on your tail. I was in the hotel lobby and saw you through the window, and I'd like to never catch up to you."

Breanna felt the sting of sudden tears.

Ma seemed to see it. She didn't embrace Breanna, which would've brought them on. She laced her arm through Breanna's elbow and fell into step beside her. "You're exhausted. Let's go and get you cleaned up. I'll shuffle the rest of them away so you can rest."

Breanna felt the exhaustion in every fiber of her being. But—"I don't think I can sleep."

Ma looked at her. And seemed to know it wasn't the race adrenaline that was keeping her up. "There's a little cafe down the corner. Let's grab a cup of coffee and a moment without your pa listening to every word."

Breanna allowed Ma to tow her to the glass-windowed establishment. Smells of fresh-baked goods and strong coffee assaulted her.

Ma found a pair of empty stools at the counter in the back, and Breanna slumped onto one of them.

She barely even noticed a waitress approach and fill their coffee mugs. Ma offered a hushed, "Thanks."

Breanna curled her hands around the mug, letting the coffee's heat seep into her.

"What happened with your young man?" Ma asked. No preamble. Just straight out.

"Nothing," Breanna said. "I found him in the livery. With his family. And I..." She sighed.

"Ran away again?"

Ma's gentle words stung.

"Adam called me a coward in Iowa." She'd been angry then. Denied it.

But maybe he was right.

Ma settled one hand over Breanna's wrist. She still hadn't drunk a drop of her coffee.

"When I first met you," Ma said, "I found you shocking."

Breanna had been young, too young to understand the adults around her. But she could well imagine what the prim and proper Penny had felt back then.

"We were hooligans," she admitted. "Me most of all." She'd always been trying to catch up to her brothers.

"Not that," Ma said. "It was your courage. You weren't afraid to ride a fifteen-hand horse—even though you should've been," she said with a firm set to her lips. "Or to climb onto the roof. Or scuffle with a bully at school. You were fearless."

Breanna shook her head. Maybe she had been at one time.

Ma squeezed her arm. "I should've said something after our Philadelphia trip three years ago."

Breanna was careful not to let anything show in her expression. "What do you mean?"

"After you confronted them. Was it your mother?"

Breanna looked up at her in shock. It was a moment before she could speak. "Grandfather. I think. How did you—?"

Ma smiled a little. "You have always worn your heart on your sleeve—and in your expression." Ma shook her head. "You and Cecilia were thick as thieves, and you seemed fine. And I was… relieved, I guess. Not to have to talk about it. I'm sorry. I should've reassured you then."

Breanna closed her eyes. "Why didn't they want me?" she whispered.

"It was never about you," Ma said. She rubbed Breanna's back, a soothing touch. "It was always about them. Their selfishness. Their desires." There was a definite note of tears in her voice as she went on. "They missed out on a chance to know what a beautiful, brave, caring girl you are. And maybe it makes me selfish, but I'm glad we didn't have to share you with them."

Breanna laughed, but it was soggy.

There were a few moments of silence between them. She tried to figure out how to ask the right question. What should she do about Adam?

Somehow, Ma knew. "Don't let one awful family represent the entire upper class of a city," she said. "When I was in finishing school, I knew several girls from families that were nothing like the Broadhursts."

Breanna swiped a tear from her cheek. "What if— what if I see them?" What if they were rude to her in public? Or she embarrassed Adam?

"You could ignore them," Ma said. "Or show them kindness. Whatever felt right to you. They aren't anything to you. *We* are your family. And Adam, if you choose him. They are irrelevant."

Ma's words were like a balm to her soul. Breanna was well-loved. She'd never wanted for anything. Never questioned Pa's love for her, and later Ma's.

But what had happened with Mr. Broadhurst had made her question whether Adam could love her without question.

He'd proved it, hadn't he? Giving up his last ride for her. Giving her the chance to decide. Knowing her, knowing all her secrets, and letting her know all of his.

"I'm in love with him," she whispered to Ma, tears pooling.

"I know." Ma patted her back. "Your Pa even thinks he might be halfway good enough for you."

Breanna laughed again. For years, she'd prided herself on never crying. Today, she was a mess. She blamed the lack of sleep, the elation and the desolation of the morning.

"I need to find Adam." She turned on the barstool, then froze in place. He was just inside the cafe door.

With his brother and the well-dressed woman beside him.

16

"**A** *dam.*"

He saw the word cross her lips, though he couldn't hear her above the noise of other diners or the pounding of his heart in his ears.

She was here.

She hadn't disappeared on him.

Nothing was settled, but he still had a chance.

She crossed the room, rounding tables and side-stepping a waitress. And then he saw her mother just behind her. He glanced around, but the place was empty of her other family members.

Was it a good or bad sign that Breanna had taken time to be with her mother just after the race's completion?

His pulse thundered as she neared.

He couldn't help it. He reached out for her. She met his hand, and he clasped his palm around hers.

Suddenly, everything felt right in the world.

"I believe congratulations are in order."

She glowed, her smile both bright and shy. She was still trail-worn and covered in dust, but he barely noticed. "Thank you. I never would have made it without your stallion. He's incredible."

He squeezed her hand. "It took your skill as a rider to bring it out in him. I'm proud of you."

A soft flush suffused her cheeks. He wanted to congratulate her properly, but this wasn't the place.

"You remember my mother?" she said softly.

He found himself pulled into a hug by the auburn-haired beauty.

"Thank you for taking care of her," Penny murmured into his shoulder.

He laughed. "The truth is, I would've been lost out there without her. Utterly lost."

Reggie laughed, and Adam was reminded of his manners.

"May I introduce my brother, Reggie, and his fiancée, Miranda Peters? This is Penny White. And this... is Breanna."

Breanna smiled, but Adam felt the tension she carried in her lower back with the hand he'd rested there.

Reggie's smile was natural. "I only know the basics, and that is that my brother is smitten with you." He held out his hand, and Breanna took it, a blush rising in her cheeks.

"It's lovely to meet you," she murmured. "Adam told me about you."

Reggie quirked a smile, and there was only a hint of pain there.

He'd changed so much since Adam had last spoken to him, maybe a week before the race. Reggie was at peace.

Breanna shook Miranda's hand, her smile tense.

"Have you eaten?" Adam asked. "We were going to get breakfast."

"And talk," Reggie added. He wasn't going to let this *being the editor-in-chief* business go. "You should join us." His smile at Adam carried a hint of the mischief from their childhood.

Breanna and her mother exchanged a look. Adam saw Penny reach out and squeeze her daughter's hand.

"I'll stay."

And he and Penny were the only ones who knew how much it cost Breanna to say the words.

"I'll see you back at the hotel." Penny disappeared outside, and a waitress pointed them to a square table in the back corner of the restaurant.

How was Reggie supposed to maneuver the chair all the way over there? There were people seated at the scattered tables throughout, their chairs pushed back and making it almost impossible.

Adam wouldn't have thought to do it, but Miranda cleared the way for Reggie's chair by speaking to several people. Her gentle smile and kindness smoothed the way, but by the time they'd reached the table and Adam had removed one of the chairs so that Reggie could wheel right up to the table, his brother's face was flushed, his knuckles white.

Adam didn't know how to make it better for him. He felt no embarrassment about his brother's condition, but it was obvious that Reggie hated having to ask for special accommodations.

Miranda seated herself, and her hand fell to Reggie's arm with a natural grace. It didn't seem planned or even that she'd registered that Reggie needed to be comforted—though surely she must've recognized his unease. She made it seem as if she just wanted to touch him.

Reggie took a deep breath, and Adam watched his tension drain away.

Miranda leaned forward to engage Breanna. "Your ride had the crowd on their feet. You were really flying."

Breanna's knee bounced beneath the table. "I wasn't sure Domino had it in him. With so few riders left and the delay from Buster going lame, I wasn't sure how near we were to first place. Not until the sun started coming up."

Adam had naturally angled his chair toward hers and now used the opportunity to slide his boot across the floor until he could nudge hers.

Her gaze slid to his.

He made his voice grave. "I'm going to have to tell Domino you doubted him."

She laughed and shook her head. "I still can't believe he had that last little push in him."

Adam tapped her boot with his. "I told you."

"Too bad you didn't wager on *him*," she murmured. Then she turned to Reggie. "How did you find the journey? Adam had mentioned you were homebound."

"Difficult." Reggie admitted it with a wry shake of his head. "But not impossible. If only I could leave my pride behind." He glanced at Adam before focusing on her again. "I suppose I had to prove to myself that I could accomplish it before I could ask my brother to believe in what I can do."

She shook her head, uncomprehending.

Adam leaned back slightly in his chair. "Reggie wants to run the *Explorer*. He's apparently always dreamed of taking over Father's job."

"I'd given up on the idea until Miranda rubbed my face in my self-pity as if I were a puppy who'd messed on the carpet."

Breanna stifled a giggle while Miranda pretended affront.

"I did not do that."

Reggie looked at her, his affection clear on his face. "You didn't have to. You gave that little disapproving sniff—that one, yes thank you for the demonstration—every time I sulked. Which was all the time," he told Breanna. "It didn't take me long to realize that if someone as intelligent and vital as Miranda believed I could be something, that maybe I should start believing in myself again too."

Breanna raised her coffee mug to him. "It takes a smart man to recognize that his woman is always right. And you were smart enough to ask her to marry you."

Reggie slid a glance to Adam. "I've always been the smart one."

Heat sliced up Adam's neck and into his face with painful intensity. Maybe having Reggie back in his life in a meaningful way wasn't as great of an idea as he'd thought.

Breanna only laughed. "You remind me of my brother Matty. I have to say I'm delighted to know you."

It seemed that she remained delighted as they enjoyed a leisurely breakfast. They were loitering at the table as the cafe emptied of its breakfast crowd, the two women distracted and conversing in low tones when Reggie leaned toward Adam.

"Miranda was right," he said. "About you being the family's legacy. When I saw that photograph in the Chicago paper, I was inspired. You had this look about you. Well, I can't describe it, but you were determined to win."

On that first day, he had been—determined to win Breanna.

"My first trip out of the house was to Father's office," Reggie continued. "I bribed Clarence to send me a copy of your telegraphs before they made it to print. I had to know about the race. How you were faring. *That's* your talent. Inspiring people—with your words, and yourself."

Adam laughed outright. "All right, you flatterer." He held his hands up in front of him. "I surrender. You've convinced me. I'll speak to Father with you, and we'll see where it goes."

Reggie lit up. Adam hadn't even known that his spirit had been dark until his excitement shone out of his eyes.

Breanna looked over at them, though she was drooping over her empty coffee mug.

Adam wasn't much better. Exhaustion had set in hours ago. "Let's walk back to your parents' hotel. You need to sleep. Reg, Miranda. If you'll excuse us."

Breanna wobbled a bit as she got to her feet. "Muscles locked up," she murmured as he steadied her with a hand at her waist.

It was as good an excuse as any to offer his arm, and she took it, leaning into him as they stepped out onto the sidewalk.

He could get used to this.

If she'd agree.

Breanna closed her eyes as she and Adam emerged out onto the sidewalk. The sunlight—though it filtered down between two buildings—felt good on her face.

Adam squeezed her arm against his side. "Don't fall asleep yet. You've a real bed waiting for you just down the street."

She hummed and opened her eyes. "It sounds lovely." She shot him a sideways glance. "So does you not being chained to your father's desk. What will you do?"

He shook his head, a bemused smile on his face. "I don't know. I was so shocked to see Reggie in the crowd this morning that I've kept pinching myself. It doesn't seem real."

She was close enough to detect his inhale and the way it seemed to catch in his chest. "Out there"—he waved vaguely toward the west—"with so much time to think, of course I imagined what it would be like to choose a different path. A different life. But I never thought it could be a real possibility."

He went silent as they squeezed through a throng of people waiting to pass at a street corner.

He cleared his throat. "I was expecting you at the livery. Not that I'm not happy to have run into you at the cafe. I was just wondering—"

"If I had run away again? So you can call me a coward again?"

He grimaced. "I'll always regret saying that to you. I didn't know—"

"Of course you didn't. I only found out this morning that Ma knew."

He looked at her sharply. "You spoke about it?"

"She... set me straight, I suppose."

They were nearing the hotel, but she wasn't ready to go inside. Not quite yet. She stopped walking and turned to face him on the sidewalk. "Adam. Ask me to come back to Philadelphia with you."

His gaze was wary even as he took both her hands in his. "How do you know I won't go back to Bear Creek? I liked it there during the one day I spent with your family."

His wry statement brought a smile, but she had to remain focused. "Even if your brother takes over, there will be business to settle at the paper, won't there? And your father needs you."

He shook his head slightly. "I don't want you to be unhappy."

She squeezed his hands. "Adam. Ask me."

He stared at her for a long moment and then let go of her left hand as his right reached into his vest.

Then he dropped to one knee right there on the sidewalk.

Passersby turned and gawked .

She heard a familiar voice from several yards away, probably right in front of the hotel. Seb, calling out, "What're you doing, City Slicker?"

She ignored it, and Adam did too.

Right now she didn't care if the whole mess of them were standing on the sidewalk watching.

Because Adam—

He drew a deep breath, and she felt the tremor that went through his hand still clasping hers.

"Come back to Philadelphia with me," he said. His gaze was intense, unrelenting. "I love you. I can't imagine my life without you in it. Whether we'll stay in Philadelphia or end up back in Bear Creek or go on an adventure somewhere else entirely, I don't know. But I do know that I want to be with you wherever life takes us. Will you marry me?"

A single tear slipped down her cheek. She nodded. "Yes."

And then he stood, slipped the ring onto her finger, and swept her into his arms.

She met his kiss eagerly, knowing they were causing a stir on the sidewalk. More so when several cowboy whoops went up from yards away. Her brothers.

Adam smiled against her lips. He broke away to finger the a delicate gold band with a beautiful white, fiery stone in the center that he'd given her.

"It's an opal. It was my grandmother's."

"I love you," she whispered, because she hadn't said it yet, and it needed to be said. She was humbled when his eyes got conspicuously wet.

He kissed her again, and then they were surrounded by her family, receiving hugs for her and slaps on the back for him.

Pa shook Adam's hand as Breanna met Ma's gaze above Velma's head. Ma smiled a secret, warm smile.

And she knew, no matter where she and Adam ended up, that she'd bring her family with them. Maybe only in spirit, but she'd always be Jonas and Penny's daughter. Always have the strength they'd instilled in her by their constant love and devotion.

The same love and devotion she and Adam would pass on to their children someday.

She was passed around again for more hugs and

then intercepted by Adam, who kept his arm around her.

Looking up into his dear face, she couldn't wait for whatever adventures God had in store for them. Together.

EPILOGUE

Breanna stood outside the stall watching a mare of almost pure white as it paced the small space.

Agitation was a sure sign of impending delivery. She'd been waiting to meet this colt for weeks.

She'd been back and forth to the barn numerous times today. Barn? Maybe she should be calling it a stable. It was much bigger than any barn she'd seen back home in Converse County.

The barn door opened, and snow swirled in. Her husband blew in with it.

Husband.

After two months of marriage, it was still difficult to believe. Her, married.

"I thought I'd find you out here. I brought your supper."

She met Adam with a smile. Instead of taking the plate he held, she slipped her arms beneath his open coat and embraced him. He obliged her with a kiss, his lips and nose a cold press against her skin.

She stepped back and accepted the plate he'd covered with a towel. "Thank you."

Adam peeked in the stall. "She seems fine."

"It's getting close." She perched on a hay bale and dug into the meal of roasted chicken and vegetables.

He shot a wry glance at her. "I think you're more nervous than she is."

Breanna gave him a baleful glare as she cut another slice of chicken.

She couldn't help her excitement. Adam had introduced her to his friend Frank soon after they'd arrived in Philadelphia, and the three of them got along like pups in a basket. Frank had notified them of a mare coming up for sale, one that had been bred from a cup-winning stallion whose owner was having a bit of a financial crisis and needed to sell. Breanna had taken one look at the mare and bought her outright, spending a large chunk of her race winnings. She'd never made so large a purchase before.

And she intended to make the foal Adam's Christmas gift. As it was Christmas Eve, it would be ideal if the mare foaled oh... right about now.

"How are your father and Reggie?" Adam had made the short trek to the Cartwright's mansion in Philadelphia proper earlier in the day.

After they'd married, they'd purchased a property just outside of town. An estate really. The house was two stories and fine and had an expansive lawn and this crazy barn. And it was near enough to Frank and his racing track that they could ride over in less than an hour.

And it was close enough that Adam could check in on his father and Reggie when he needed to.

"Reggie is excelling as editor-in-chief. I never thought..." Adam shook his head.

Breanna knew there'd been tension between the brothers as Reggie had taken over the paper these past weeks. After nearly fifteen years of seeing Reggie as helpless—and Reggie doing nothing but perpetuating that image—Adam had still tried to coddle his younger brother.

It hadn't gone well.

Reggie's newfound independence had reared its head, and there'd been some squabbling. After growing up with her passel of brothers, it was nothing surprising to Breanna, but Adam had been stymied. Things had smoothed over in the past two weeks, for which everyone was thankful.

"And your father?" she asked.

He'd had a lung infection over the last week and been laid up. After his collapse during the summer, everyone in the family had been on pins and needles, worried about him.

"He's growling at everyone, and Mother is about ready to throttle him. He'll be on his feet in a day or two."

Breanna put aside the now-empty plate and stood next to Adam.

The mare was lying down now.

"I told you it was close," she murmured.

He nudged her elbow with his. "Don't you ever get tired of being right?"

She snorted. "I believe you've been right your fair share of times. Not going swimming after Scar-face. That sofa we put in the parlor." She exhaled softly. "And that I could be happy here in Pennsylvania."

He tilted his head to look down to her, his eyes warm and serious. "I was waiting for a good time to bring it up. You seem content enough. No regrets?"

She leaned her head on his shoulder. "No."

Adam had been right. She fit perfectly into his life here. He rarely attended extravagant parties. His mother had thrown a party to celebrate their wedding, and Breanna had been tempted to skip it, but she'd proved she wasn't a coward. Proved it to herself, and had had to prove it to Adam's mother's society friends.

The Broadhursts had not been present. She didn't know—and hadn't asked—whether they'd been invited. It would be just like Adam to manage things so she wouldn't have to face them.

She was no longer afraid to meet them face to face, but she wasn't going to seek them out again. Ma was right. She had a family, and they'd rallied around her, traveling across the country to witness her wedding to Adam.

She was a White, through and through. And now a Cartwright.

Adam slipped his arm around her shoulder. "I'm

glad."

"You don't want to move to Wyoming? I know you liked it there."

His jaw rested against the crown of her head, and she felt him smile. "I do like it there. Maybe we should go for a visit."

He slipped his opposite hand into his pocket and came out with two train tickets. Flipped them so she could see. "On our way to California."

"What? Adam!"

California. She'd mentioned it once in passing, barely admitted to herself that she'd like to go one day. Now he'd bought tickets?

"I thought it could be our first adventure together as man and wife."

"Are you chasing a story?"

He chuckled. "Not this time. Just trying to make my wife happy."

"I am. I'll be happier if your gift arrives before Christmas—Adam, look!"

While they'd been talking, the mare had been working. They watched now, and a few minutes later, she birthed a knobby-kneed colt.

"He takes after the stallion," Adam whispered as the mare worked to clean the foal.

It stood on shaky legs. It was arguably the most adorable thing Breanna had ever seen.

"Merry Christmas, darling."

Adam kissed the tip of her nose. "Merry Christmas, cowgirl."

ALSO BY LACY WILLIAMS

Wind River Hearts series

Marrying Miss Marshal

Counterfeit Cowboy

Cowboy Pride

The Homesteader's Sweetheart

Courted by a Cowboy

Roping the Wrangler

Return of the Cowboy Doctor

The Wrangler's Inconvenient Wife

A Cowboy for Christmas

Her Convenient Cowboy

Her Cowboy Deputy

Catching the Cowgirl

The Cowboy's Honor

Sutter's Hollow series (contemporary romance)

His Small-Town Girl

Secondhand Cowboy

The Cowgirl Next Door

Looking Back, Texas series (contemporary romance)

10 Dates

Next Door Santa

Always a Bridesmaid

Love Lessons

The Sawyer Creek series (contemporary romance)

Soldier Under the Mistletoe

The Nanny's Christmas Wish

The Rancher's Unexpected Gift

Someone Old

Someone New

Someone Borrowed

Someone Blue (newsletter subscribers only)

The Bull Rider

The Brother

The Prodigal

Cowboy Fairytales series (contemporary romance)

Once Upon a Cowboy

Cowboy Charming

The Toad Prince

The Beastly Princess

The Lost Princess

Kissing Kelsey

Courting Carrie

Stealing Sarah

Keeping Kayla

Melting Megan

Heart of Oklahoma series (contemporary romance)

Kissed by a Cowboy

Love Letters from Cowboy

Mistletoe Cowboy

Cowgirl for Keeps

Jingle Bell Cowgirl

Heart of a Cowgirl

3 Days with a Cowboy

Prodigal Cowgirl

Not in a Series

Wagon Train Sweetheart (historical romance)

Printed in Great Britain
by Amazon

23693630R00139